A Little Bit of Sinning, novel
Naked Confessions, novel

•

Ultimate Freak-fest Fantasy, novella
Sin-Sexual, novella (coming soon)

•

The Masquerade Party, short story - The New York Times Best Selling Anthology *Caramel Flava* edited by Zane

Chocolate Cream, short story - *Honey Flava* edited by Zane

Satiated Desire, short story - *Lipstick Diaries 2* edited by Anthony Whyte

Madame Travina's Diary, short story - *Lipstick Diaries 3* edited by Anthony Whyte

•

www.MissTracee.com
www.Facebook.com/TraceeAHanna

A
HEDONISTIC NOVELLA
OF
FANTASY, PASSION, AND DESIRE,
FOR
THE ENJOYMENT
OF
THE UNINHIBITED READER
OF
EXPLICITLY WRITTEN
EROTICA

Footprints

On The

Headboard

Tracee A. Hanna

Book two in The Ultimate Urban Erotica Series.

This book is a work of fiction. Names, characters, places, and incidents are either products of the author's imagination or used fictionally. Any resemblance to actual events or locales or persons, living, or dead, is entirely coincidental.

TRACEE A. HANNA
FOOTPRINTS ON THE HEADBOARD

For more information contact:
Bella Tracee Books, BellaTraceeBooks@MissTracee.com

First Edition December 2015

Image ID: 12133520 (Male Model) Copyright Lunamarina | Dreamstime.com http://www.dreamstime.com/lunamarina_info
Image ID: 37444124 (Hotel Suite) Copyright Amoklv | Dreamstime.com http://www.dreamstime.com/amoklv_info
Image ID: 11713507 (Legs) Copyright Mocker | Dreamstime.com http://www.dreamstime.com/mocker_info

Sometimes...
I just have to
give in to
Temptation

Ultimate Freak-fest Fantasy

By

Tracee A. Hanna

Book one in the Ultimate Urban Erotica Series

DEDICATION:

This book, as with my every book, is dedicated to the most exquisite ladies I have had the pleasure of meeting in my life, my daughters, Rebecca and Monique. Thank you for being the best children I could ever ask God for. I love you two with all of my heart.

ACKNOWLEDGEMENTS:

I would like to give a special thank you and God be with you always to my daughter Rebecca H., your contribution to Bella Tracee Books is priceless. Thank you so very much Edwina H. and Lisa R. for you willingness to read my work. I appreciate your honest opinions and noteworthy feedback. And last but certainly not least, hello to all of the men I have met over the years you made life really entertaining and for that I solute you.

CONTENTS:

CHAPTER ONE
CARNIVAL DE BELLA

Female orgasms are as varied as they are mysterious. There is however a key ingredient, excitement. Women cream their panties without being touched, and experience vivid wet dreams, products of their combustible passions. Sweet pleasures ignited by a spark of unexpected stimulation—sensual desire which could not and would not be contained.

Wet dreams plagued Bella every night for weeks. Reminisce of one man's sex thrilled her. A lustful Jamaican inundated her body with new tantalizing carnal pleasures. The ultimate zenith: her mind, flesh, and soul gravitated naturally to orgasm because of one special mister and his magnificent dick, or so she thought.

Bella was sure that she found the perfect lover, Roman Thompson, on a night filled with impetuousness, a complete surrender of her inhibitions. In those moments, Roman was absolutely irresistible. At first glance she saw pride, strength, confidence, and a rare echelon of masculinity bound in silky brown skin. She immediately thought: I have to have him. Roman was a tall strapping man with a lovely masculine face and the most alluring green eyes she had ever had the pleasure of gazing into. As she looked upon his face, she imagined she could spend an eternity kissing his luscious lips. I absolutely adore him, she mused. Come fuck me, make me cum over and over again big man. Damn, he is sexy as hell. I have got to know... Oh shit here he comes.

"And what's your name?" Roman asked, his brand of seduction was heightened by his Jamaican accent.

≈

Bella cried out as her eyes opened to darkness. She had been shocked awake by intense orgasmic explosions. She laid in her bed panting softly, her body practically mummified by her cum soaked sheets which immobilized her. Bella continued to stare into the shadows of the night. The same dream haunted her every night for months. "How did I get here?" Bella screeched. "Why is this happening to me?" She closed her eyes. "Someone please tell me…" Her voice trailed off into a whisper as a tear rolled down her cheek. "I'm totally mystified." The memory of the past two years of her life came flooding back.

≈

"I met someone," Samson stated serenely. The last three words Bella ever expected to hear over the phone. "I met someone," Samson stated for the second time. "She's the one Bella." He cleared his throat nervously, "Bella? Are you there? Hello…?"

Alas, she was not. Bella had placed the phone on the coffee table immediately after she heard Samson's happy news. She packed a bag and headed for the airport. No matter where Bella had traveled to over the years her hometown, St. Louis, Missouri, was the one place in the world where she could always find solace. Little did she know she was about to embark on the most spine-tingling erotically tempestuous journey that she had ever experienced, a sexual carnival if you will. Every carnival has key characters and a special guest, Carnival De Bella was no different.

Kenneth Lovejoy was young, hot, and resplendent, the fun house filled with intemperate sexual taboos. Samson Carter was the long time "homey lover friend," a thrill ride in his own right, sexually and otherwise.

Omar Kingston was the special act—a one night only—albeit an immediate encore performance. The decadent Roman Thompson was the devil incarnate, nothing more need be said. Finally of course, there was the ever pulchritudinous Bella, the carnival's queen.

Bella was a woman who loved men: big men, strong men, from businessmen to gangsters. She wantonly yielded to their power. She allowed herself to be captivated by their charm. Bella respected masculinity, boldness, strength, and authority. There was nothing one man could do or say to turn her against another. Her desire was solely based on individual character or the lack thereof. She was attracted to the alpha-male like a phoenix to the sun. She savored every explosion, and bathed in fiery pleasures, after which she was renewed. Bella's fiendish craving for salacious pleasure was her dirty little secret.

Samson was Bella's favorite person on Earth—the man with whom she could be her unabashed self. They enjoyed years of wildly experimental sexual encounters together. She knew as long as she had him in her life she would never be alone in the world, alas, their love affair could not last forever. However Bella steadfastly believed their friendship could weather any storm and last a lifetime. Unfortunately for her everything she believed to be true all changed after Samson uttered three little words, over the phone.

"I met someone..." Samson's words rang in Bella's ear—reverberated in her mind time and time again until she could not stand it anymore. "Bastardo!" she exclaimed. Bastard, one of the many Spanish words she had picked up on their trip to Spain.

Experiencing the nudist lifestyle was the last of Samson's ultimate freak-fest fantasies therefore Bella accompanied him to Vera Playa Club Hotel in Vera, Spain. Bella became quite comfortable on the beach as she openly enjoyed penis watching, a perk that Samson had not foreseen. Apparently his pre-vacation imaginings were solely focused on tits and ass. His dissatisfaction was made quite clear from his grumblings.

"Did you really think you'd be the only man here?" Bella asked offhandedly as she continued her sport. "Cute," she giggled.

Bella recalled the last moments she and Samson spent together as she sipped her in-flight cocktail. Samson took special care in saying his goodbyes. He hugged her a little too tightly and his kiss felt strangely wistful. In fact, Samson had not quite been himself since he had woken up that fated morning. He did not make love to Bella as per their usual goodbye. Samson was fuck happy instead. He fucked her mouth and ate her pussy in bed, fucked her ass in the shower before breakfast and fucked her pussy in the crystal blue waters of Vera Playa. There she was in Europe again, just for Samson, lying on the beach wearing nothing but a sheer sarong. He was completely nude. The taste of his cum was fresh in her mouth. She could feel the remnants of their last fuck between her thighs. It was in that moment of pure contentment that Samson looked over to her and smiled. Even his smile said a strange goodbye.

"What is it Samson?" Bella asked teasingly. "Are you going to miss me terribly?"

"Yes I am," he said his voice uncharacteristically emotional. "We will always be friends. We will always be happy for one another, right Bella?"

"Of course we will Samson," she softly kissed his lips before continuing. "We love each other."

"I do love you Bella." He gathered her in his arms. "How much longer are you staying?"

I'm not sure, I bought an open ticket. I don't have to be in Saint Louis until next week and Vera Playa Club Hotel is an all-inclusive resort so…"

"The room is paid for 'til the end of the week."

"Thank you sweetness, I'll book a suite if I decide to stay longer."

"I am proud of your success Bella. I wish you nothing but the best." Samson took a deep breath. "My train back to Italy leaves in an hour. Stay here, relax, and have another cocktail. I'll call you when I get home."

"I'm proud of you too Samson. You're climbing up in rank like a mountaineer. The United States Air Force is lucky to have you. I can't believe you are leaving three days early. Whatever is taking you away from me had better be a matter of national security."

"It's very important," Samson stated adamantly. He kissed Bella goodbye.

A few hours later Samson called. "I met someone…" Although Bella knew the day would come, she was ill prepared. The beauty of Spain was lost on her from that moment on. She wanted to go home. She refused to listen to Samson's words, refused to hear to him confess his love for another woman. The three words he uttered were more than enough. The words haunted her. She could not run away fast enough.

Bella finished out her book tour. A few months later she landed in St. Louis once more. She was happy to be in her hometown. She checked into her favorite hotel overlooking the Mississippi River. As she showered flashes of the last sex she and Samson indulged in whipped through her minds eye. "He fucked me goodbye!" she cried out. "Oh God… That's not love, that's not even friendship. Who the fuck does that?" Bella dried her face before wrapping the towel around her body. She looked into the mirror, cocked her head to the side and said, "I don't have time for this shit. I'm in the Lou and the malls are open. It's time to get my retail therapy on," she exclaimed.

Bella had the car service drop her off on Laclede's Landing, her childhood happy place. Laclede's Landing was a popular vintage locale in St. Louis, Missouri, located just north of the Eads Bridge on the Mississippi Riverfront. The multi-block area boasted cobblestone streets and epoch brick and cast-iron warehouses dating back to the mid 1800s. The old buildings had been converted into shops, restaurants, and bars. Bella was on the hunt for some good ole Saint Louis style barbeque ribs and an ice cold Budweiser.

No sooner than she walked into a restaurant a woman called out her name. Bella's eyes panned the room as she slowly walked towards the hostess podium all the while wondering who had recognized her, family, friend, or fan.

"Bella!" the woman called out again as she made her way to the front of the restaurant.

"Kathryn," Bella said warmly. They smiled brightly as they instantly embraced. "I can't believe it's you." Bella held Kathryn's hands as she looked into her eyes. "How have you been? How's our son?"

Bella's last question was rewarded with a strange look from the hostess. The ladies laughed openly as they walked away together. Bella joined Kathryn for a beer at the bar. Kathryn was Bella's former employer and long time friend. Bella was her babysitter for five years. The child, Kenneth Lovejoy, had long since grown into a man.

"Please join me for lunch," Bella invited.

"I have a better idea. I'm throwing a party tonight at my house and I would love it if you could make an appearance." Kathryn said. "I'm only here to pick up the wings and veggie platters. The real food is back at the house."

"I'm down," Bella all but shouted, "and if you feed me some of them wings I'll help you cook."

"You know I love your cooking!" Kathryn beamed with joy. "You haven't changed a bit. A lot of people get successful and forget where they came from."

"It's been a long time since I've been to the old neighborhood but family is family and we share a son."

Bella made herself at home in Kathryn's kitchen. She prepared her famous spicy brown sugar and bacon baked beans all the while Kathryn sat at the tabling across from her shucking corn. The ladies talked and laughed about the different paths their lives had taken. Kathryn stared at Bella as her heart filled with joy and her eyes filled with tears.

"Bella you haven't changed one bit," Kathryn said again happily. "I'm so glad I ran into you after all these years," she continued. She reached over and hugged her. "I'm glad you stuck to writing. I brag about you, you know." Bella turned to the stove bashfully although inside she beamed with pride. Kathryn went back to shucking corn. "I have a surprise for you."

"Really... What kind of a surprise?" Bella asked.

"My son is home from college. He just graduated last month."

"You don't say? I haven't seen that boy since he was eighteen or nineteen. How old is he now?"

"He just turned twenty-two two weeks ago."

"Is he that old already?"

"Yes, he is an independent adult now. Thank God!"

"I know he has grown into a fine young man. What time will he be here?"

"I sent him to the store for some more beer. He should be back any minute now, if he isn't here all ready. Why don't you go downstairs and look."

"I can't wait to see him again." Bella stated although she remained.

"Woman go on downstairs, you are his surprise."

"Oh okay. Why didn't you just say so?"

Bella tiptoed down the basement steps and there was Kenneth unloading the beer into an old refrigerator. She tapped him on the shoulder.

"Hey could you hand me a cold one please?" she asked.

"Sure, what kind?" he responded without taking pause from his task.

"What ever you grab is fine."

"Here you go." He reached back with bottle of Bud Light.

"Thank you but can you open it, please?"

"Yeah, sure," he stood up straight. He twisted the cap off using his shirt. "Here you go ma'am." He finally turned and looked down at her. She smiled up at him. "Bella? Naw man! Is that really you Mommy?"

"Yes Love, its me." she reached for him as he reached for her. Bella's eyes closed tight as she laid her head on his chest, as did his when he placed his cheek on top of her head. "How's my baby doing?" She asked, her face buried in the bend of his arm.

"I've missed you Mommy." He held on tight. They stood there locked in a warm embrace for quite some time. "I'm so glad you're here." He tightened his grip on her. "You are exactly what I need."

Bella leaned back and looked into his eyes again. He had gotten much taller since the last time she saw him. Kenneth was magnificently built. He was a fair complexioned black man who stood six feet and two inches tall. He had naturally curly hair and a dimpled smile.

"What's wrong Baby?" she asked, however he didn't respond. He kissed her affectionately on the lips. "Oh my sweet baby… I'm here for you. Tell me…"

"Everything Mommy, everything," he stated emotionally.

"Do you want to talk about it now or after the party?"

"I don't even feel like being here."

"Listen Baby, life is hard. There's always something that comes along to throw you for a loop. How you deal with situations is what makes or breaks you."

"You're so right Mommy."

"Come on now, let's finish loading the beer, so we can go outback and get our drink on."

"That sounds good to me." He smiled into Bella's eyes before releasing her. "How long are you going to be here anyway?"

"I don't know…" she said as she waved her beer in the air. "But I do know that I have no intentions of being too sober while I'm here. I have to maintain my level of inebriation for the duration."

"What are you drinking on?"

"Jack Daniels with a Bud back," she said as she lifted up her beer and read the label. "Make that a Bud Light."

"Awe shit, you are going to have a good time tonight."

"Hell yeah!"

"I ain't go'n let nobody get at you Mommy. You're all mine."

Kenneth had grown into a strong man, although at that point Bella still viewed him as her sweet baby—the little boy she use to look after. She didn't mind him keeping close to her that evening. Bella had not realized it yet but she needed Kenneth as well.

The party was jumping and the drinks flowed freely. There were good looking men in attendance however no one really caught Bella's attention although some tried. Unfortunately for Bella she accepted an invitation to dance from Theodore Black. After the dance he boldly sat at her table yet Bella remained standing. She looked at Kenneth and smiled before she turned her attention to Mr. Black.

"Theodore," Bella began reluctantly, "this is Ken…"

"I already know little Kenny," Theodore interjected. His thick lip grin perfectly framed pink and black gums and horse teeth. "Call me Black," he said with a wink before directing his gaze onto Kenneth, "Yeah, lil' Kenny and I go way back, ABCs and 123s. Ain't that right lil' Kenny Ken?"

"I'm going to um, go get a drink." Bella said as she slowly backed away from the table. "You two catch up."

"Why don't you stay right here with me? Come on now Baby-girl we are both beautiful people, why can't we get together and have," Black paused. He looked over at Kenneth before finishing his sentence, "some grown up fun?"

Footprints On The Headboard

Bella looked into Black's eyes with a devilish grin she said, "Some grown up fun hmm?" Bella's voice was sugar sweet. Kenneth sat back in his chair and relaxed. Let the head games begin, he thought totally amused. Bella took a seat directly across from Black. "So, you think you can rock with me?"

"Awe yeah Baby-girl..." Black misinterpreted her demeanor. He smiled and sucked his teeth like a wolf that had finally cornered its prey. "You and me, we can get a room together suga'."

"A room... You can't take me back to your place?"

"I can take you to my place but I was thinking that if we went to a room we could uh, you know, do the damn thang."

"Oh!" Bella faked surprised excitement. "So you want to do it up like that?"

"Ooh yeah Baby-girl."

"Why don't you tell me what kind of things you want to do to me?"

"I want to lick your honey pot Baby-girl. I bet you got that good-good, juicy."

"I do, it's hot, wet, succulent." Bella slid her foot up Black's leg. "I'm getting turned on just thinking about a nice looking man eating my cookies for dessert," she said although she thought: Not you... Never that. Ain't no way in hell.

"Why don't you leave this youngster alone so that I can get to know you better?"

"No, no, no." Bella's smile widened. "Now that would not be fair. I haven't given him the chance to tell me what he has to offer." She turned to Kenneth and asked, "Whatchu got for me Baby?"

"I don't have a lot of words but... I can show you," he emphasized as he reached over, took her hand and lightly trailed it across the length of his cock. Bella snatched her hand away. All the while Kenneth smiled proudly. "Is that enough for you Mommy?"

A slight frown wrinkled her brow as she stared into Kenneth's eyes, her mind a flutter. When the hell did he get all that dick? Damn! Bella was painfully aware of her pussy. Pure desire danced in her eyes, although only for a moment, Kenneth noticed. Bella quickly checked herself before she continued on with her little game.

"Oh my," she replied with southern finesse, her Machiavellian smile restored. She turned her attention to Black once more. "It's true…" She helplessly nodded her head, "He didn't have to say much."

"I have skills that this here, boy, haven't even learned yet." Black stated heatedly.

"Really?" Bella asked before she looked to Kenneth. "What about you Baby? You got something better than years of experience?"

"Stamina," Kenneth retorted smoothly.

"Damn you—" Black began loudly.

"Okay, all right, there is only one way to settle this." Bella licked her lips, looked from one man to the other, and smiled a sexy sinful smile. "I have a question and which ever one of you knows the correct answer can have me for the night."

"For the night?" posed Black. "When I get a hold of you it won't be just for one night, that's for damn sure."

"Only if you are talented enough to make me want to come back," Bella stated sarcastically. "Well actually, you have to be astute enough to get me to go with you in the first place."

"Hey Baby-girl, what if we both know the answer?" Black asked.

"Well then, I'll have to come up with a different way of choosing," Bella said as she thought: Either way I'm definitely not choosing you, playa.

"I met you first so I think I should go first." Black interjected.

"All right, you have five seconds to respond. Okay?"

"Bet!" the men retorted on cue.

"Black, Kenneth, what is my name?" Bella looked at Black and smiled. She stared passionately into Blacks eyes and began counting. "One second, two second, three second, four second, five second..." she paused for a moment longer, took a long finishing sip of her beer, licked her lips and said, "Time's up." She smiled a 'too bad so sad' smile at him before she turned to Kenneth however before could even focus on Kenneth's face Black slapped the top of the table, which brought her attention back to him. "What is your problem?" she asked, perturbed.

"Wait! That was too fast Baby-girl. I mean damn! Give a brotha a chance." Kenneth laughed. "What's so funny son?" Black asked bitterly. "You've been calling Baby-girl, "Mommy" all night." Kenneth didn't respond he just smiled smugly which spurred Black on. "Oh since you think you know so much junior, what's her name?"

"Her name is Bella." Kenneth said, and smiled arrogantly. "Am I right Mommy? Isn't your name Bella?"

"Yes you are correct. You win!"

"Ain't that a bitch," exclaimed Black and abruptly stormed out.

"Come here Baby," said Bella as she opened her arms to Kenneth. "Come on over here to Mommy and give me a hug." They both laughed as they embraced. "That was too much fun Kenny."

"How did you know he didn't know your name?"

"He never said it—never once—not even when he said hello."

"Really?" he asked amused.

"Yes, we were introduced by your mother shortly after I arrived. Instead of saying hello Bella he said hello Baby-girl, as if my name didn't matter, although he made a point of telling me to call him Black instead of Theodore. I took note right away."

"Damn. I'm going to have to remember that one."

"You played along well, why?"

"I know the way you are… how badly you treat men. For years, I wanted to witness it first hand without being on the receiving end—sensual evil."

"I am not evil," she said with a smile.

"Yes you are." Kenneth kissed Bella again. "Just not to me… Is there anyone else you're nice to—any other man?"

"Yes there was one however I don't want to talk about him."

"Who, your husband?" he asked knowingly.

"No. I'm divorced."

"Damn! Come on let's get out of here."

"And go where?"

"With me Mommy," he smiled, took Bella by the hand, and pulled her to her feet. "Let's go… I won you, remember?"

Kenneth grabbed a bottle of Jack on the way out of the door. He took Bella to his hotel room. They settled in on the couch. Old jam R&B music played softly in the back ground as they sipped their cocktails.

"So tell me Baby," Bella began, "why are you at a hotel?"

"My mother has everybody and their cousins up in the house so I had to bounce. It's all good though because my apartment will be ready on Monday."

"Oh okay. Are you working or are you still looking?"

"I'm working Mommy. I have a good job. They recruited me right out of college."

"I'm proud of you my baby; my sweet-sweet baby."

"So Mommy, tell me about this man that has your kindness."

"That ain't none of your business."

"Is he why you're here?"

"He's one of the reasons but not the only reason. My children are grown and living on their own. For the first time in my whole life I stand alone. It's just me now therefore I'm taking this time to adjust and center myself before I have to go back and face my reality."

"So you are single?" he asked enunciating ever syllable.

"Yes, my divorce will be final next month."

"When was the last time you were with a man?"

"Why are you filled with these kinds of questions sweetheart?"

"I'm a man now Mommy." Kenneth stated with a proud smile. "You just might need some maintenance."

"Oh really now?" Bella laughed out loud. "I'm all right."

"So tell me about this man Bella."

"There's nothing to tell. He kind of tiptoed into my heart when I was not looking and at the most inopportune time possible for both of us. I was married, too dedicated to my children and starting a new career and he is too busy for words."

"What, you fell for a playa?"

"If you can believe that one…"

"You Bella," Kenneth began perplexed, "you of all people?"

"Yes me. But I haven't lost my mind or done anything stupid besides have a little sex with him a few times over the years. The problem is, I have a kindness for him that I have never had for anyone else before. He reminds me of better days. Most of the time it feels like I'm living out a fantasy. I can't even be mad at him, although he has pissed me off a few times. I seem to get over it quickly, too quickly. Sometimes I even laugh. The sad part is, I miss him."

"Daaamn, you really do care for him?"

"Yes, but it's not what you think."

"What—you're not in love?"

"No, I'm not. I do care for him a lot, but it's not the kind of love where I can't live without him. It's more of the kind of affection which allows me to wish him well no matter where life takes him, miss him when we stay apart too long, and worry about him when he stays out of touch. I want him to be happy. There's just one little problem."

"What?"

"For me, sexually we are an almost perfect match."

"How do you know that?"

"I wasn't a virgin when I met him and there has been one after him beside the husband."

"How many men have you been with, if you don't mind me asking?"

"Four including my soon to be ex-husband…"

"Four?" Kenneth busted out laughing. "You have the nerve to compare him the three other people and really believe that you're sprung?"

"It's not funny."

"Yes Mommy, this right here is very funny." He laughed so hard his body began to spasm and his eyes broke into tears. "I thought you were really in love or something."

"I told you, I'm not in love. He was my lover and my friend both during my marriage and after I filed for divorce. He's military and it was easy when he didn't live close by however he going to be stationed at Luke again soon. I don't want to talk about this Baby." Kenneth sobered quickly. He took Bella into his arms and held her tight. "I need my drink," Bella said as she pulled away. She stood abruptly and he swiftly followed suit.

"I'll refresh your drink Mommy."

She looked over her shoulder yet not into his eyes and said, "Ice please."

"Yes of course."

"Thank you."

Change is rarely easy especially when it is de rigueur (strictly required), she mused.

CHAPTER TWO
NO TURNING BACK

Kenneth was on the hunt and Bella was his prey. He stalked her with his words. "Let me show you Mommy. Let me show you what good dick really is. I'm go'n help you get over this shit," Kenneth said as he walked up from behind Bella and gathered her in his arms once more. "Your drink Mommy…"

"What?" asked Bella momentarily perplexed by his touch. "Looky here Baby, how the hell are you trying to dick me down, yet still call me Mommy?"

"I'm going to make you cum all over this room while I call you Mommy," he whispered in her ear as he tightened his grip around her waist. The heat of his breath on her neck intensified her desire. "I'm going to seduce you into submission."

Yes! Bella thought immediately before clear reason prevailed. "Damn it Kenneth!" Shocked by her own response, Bella pulled away. "This is wrong on so many levels." She faced him. "Baby…"

"Come here." Kenneth pulled her to him. "I've been waiting for as long as I can remember…" He cupped her face in his hands and kissed her soundly. "Let me help you forget about everything that troubles you." His kiss deepened, "Forget everyone who hurt you," he whispered before his lips devoured hers, "at least while you are here with me." He looked into her eyes his carnal intent was ever present.

"Hold on!" Bella exclaimed as she thought: What the hell is happening here? Am I in an erotic twilight zone?

"What?" he asked boldly, his lust for her blazed like a beacon in the night.

"Wait a minute now," Bella put her hands up as she took a step back. "This would change everything between us. I would have to view you in an extremely different light…"

"Okay then… Let me help you." Kenneth said confidently. He flexed his muscles as he pulled his shirt over his head. "I'm a man Bella," he said as he stood gloriously before her.

"This is a terrible idea," Bella said as she stared at his chiseled chest. Flashes of her tongue and lips on his flesh danced in her mind's eye. Kenneth swayed his body to the music as he unfastened his belt. He stepped out of his shoes and pants all the while he smiled roguishly into her eyes. I mean hot damn. If I were ever to lay claim to a character flaw, my vulnerability to seduction would be it… Desire, lust, passion and temptation, may God have mercy on my epicurean soul, she dared to pray, all the while concupiscence consumed her.

"You like what you see Mommy, I can tell." Kenneth licked his lips. "Your eyes have always given you away." He kissed her quickly. "Tonight you will beg me to fuck you."

"Oh my…" she sighed. That's new, Bella thought slightly amused by his machismo. "You're going to make me beg?"

"Hell yeah," Kenneth stated with confidence. "If I'm right about you Mommy, you will beg."

"Why do you want me to beg for dick?" she asked half thrilled at the prospect of a man making her supplicate.

"Not for dick, for my dick." Kenneth corrected. "If you beg me to make love to you I'll know you're not thinking about another man while we are together. No man wants to be another man's stand in."

"I see." Bella allowed her eyes to molest his body. "I like the way you think Baby."

"There's one more reason Mommy," he said as he caressed her cheek.

"Really and what reason is that?" she asked. "I'm eager to know."

"I want you to want me as much as I want you." His honesty afforded her a glimpse of his vulnerability and the depth of his love before his youthful enthusiasm returned. Kenneth smiled as he did a quick twist with his hips. His penis batted back and forth beneath the cloth of his boxers from hip to hip. "I see you looking at him Mommy, and just to think, he ain't even hard yet."

"Say what," Bella blurted out before she regained her composure. "You're too young to have all that dick." she teased. "Are you sure you know what to do with that?"

"Why don't you be the judge? Take your place as a woman tonight Bella, and I'll show you."

"Alright Kenneth," Bella all but cooed. She took a seat and smiled up at him. "I acquiesce. Tell me what you like."

"Touch me Mommy." Kenneth took her hands into his. "Kiss me." He snatched her up, gathered her in his arms and kissed her hard. "I want you tonight." He bent her backwards as he slowly trailed kisses from her neck into the valley of her breasts and back again. He kneeled before her and looked up into her eyes." I've wanted this for such a long time…" Kenneth wrapped his arms around Bella's waist, placed his head on her stomach and held her tight. He stated humbly, "Stop me now if you're not down. Once I start on you I will not quit until I have you're trembling beneath me completely out of breath thanking God I finally came, yet somehow wanting more."

"No one likes a quitter." Bella said. Her pussy pulsated hard enough to make her stager back a step. She closed her eyes and wrapped her arms around Kenneth's head. Oh hell yeah! Now that right there is exactly what I need. I need to lose control. I need be conquered by the primal powers of a man—she thought although she said, "Make me beg Sweet Baby. I need to—" Bella took a deep breath. She let it out slowly as she shook her head in disbelief. She took his face in her hands and looked into his eyes. She willed him to understand her completely when she said, "Follow your desires Baby and I will follow mine."

"You won't say stop?" he asked attentively.

"No I will not," Bella affirmed. "I'll take my place." She curtsied teasingly. Kenneth removed his boxers as he stood up. His dick drizzled wet with sweet desire. "Oh my," she sighed as she thought: He is so naked… so virile.

Bella's musings continued as he rocked his pelvis back and forth and around in circles. Yes-yes! Make that dick dance for me baby. Wow, his dick swirled a figure eight. Bella was on fire yet Kenneth turned up the heat. He watched her ardor rise as he gyrated. Once his cock was hard as steel it stood straight up in a rigid salute. His pre-cum glided down his shaft. Her body helplessly leaned closer to him as her lips parted. I want to taste his excitement, she contemplated. He moved closer, within her reach.

"Kenneth," whispered Bella. She slowly reached for him yet her feet would not move, as if they were nailed to the floor.

Kenneth took her by the hand and promenaded around her body. He caressed her breast as he removed her shirt and squeezed her ass along the way. He palmed her pussy through her jeans before he moved his hand up to her waist. He looked into her eyes as he unfastened her button and lowered the zipper. Kenneth slowly slid Bella's pants down. He placed tiny kisses across her pelvis as he went. Bella fought the needed to join in given that she was determined to follow his lead.

"You turn me on Mommy," Kenneth declared. Bella stood before him wearing pink four inch strappy stiletto sandals and a matching g-string. "Turn around, bend over and touch your toes," he commanded and she obeyed, although she could not help but to giggle a little bit. Once in position, she felt warm air flowing up and down her delta followed by a hot tongue. Kenneth traced her g-string with his tongue. "Stand up straight Mommy, put you hands on your hips, and spread your legs a little more," he instructed.

Kenneth nudged his head through her legs—still tracing the outline of her undergarment with his tongue. He slipped back through her legs, gripped her thighs, and snatched her g-string off with his teeth. Bella gasped with elation. He kissed her pussy lips, and as he licked the full length of her slit she opened to him like a flower blooming on a warm spring morning. He nestled his mouth against her flesh and attacked her clitoris with his tongue and teeth nibbling and licking fervently. Her thighs tightened as he dined on her deserts. Her body quickened as he licked and sucked her prepuce teasing her relentlessly. He attached her clitoris once more lapping and sucking until she cried out. Her cries of ecstasy filled the room. Her cum splashed into his mouth and dripped down his face.

"Bounce your fat tasty pussy on my tongue Mommy." Kenneth plunged his tongue deep into her sex—she began to move. "That's it Mommy tighten your pussy muscles around my tongue and squeeze it tight."

Bella's mind raced: Oh what a sweet taboo, I've never been tongue fucked like this before. His tongue is like a little dick with taste buds, truly amazing and skilled. Kenneth paused is oral exploits only long enough to change his angle and give more instructions. "Touch your toes again Mommy." He kneeled behind her. "I love how wet you are…" He penetrated her with his tongue again. "Come on Mommy, move your ass, bump back on my tongue like you would if I were fucking you." Bella rode his tongue with vigor. Her mind clouded with passion: I love the way his tongue moves inside of my body; so sinfully wicked. Kenneth licked the little patch of skin between her pussy and anus. "Do you like that?"

"Oh sweet baby, yeeeees! Do that!" she moaned in delight.

Kenneth's tongue swooped inside of Bella's pussy yet again. Waves of pleasure coursed through her body like the waters of the ocean licks the beach on a warm sunny day. He rolled his tongue from side to side as would a slithering snake. He then flicked his tongue wildly thrashing about like a fish out of water. She moaned in elation. Bella flexed her pussy muscles and gripped his tongue tight. She tried her best to hold his tongue still for a second or two to no avail. She took pause, her breath was labored and her body glistened with sweat. She instinctively began to move again. She pushed her ass back onto his face while she gave in to their carnal need. Bella's thigh muscles tightened, her hands clutched into fists and came violently. Her juices washed over his face and down to the floor. He gave her nether lips one final kiss before he ran his tongue up the crack of her anus and he stood.

"Stand up Mommy" said Kenneth. He helped her up and spun her in his arms. His cock stood straight up against his stomach as unyielding as a concrete post. "I want you to be happy. Come play with me. Let's have some fun." He smiled gleefully.

My turn, Bella mused, she returned his smile. She wrapped her arms around is neck and pressed her body to his. She kissed his mouth ardently. She placed soft kisses all over his face. She kissed and licked his neck until he gripped her hair and pulled her away. Bella's laugh was sultry. She licked her lips and smiled up at him once more.

"Yes, let's have some fun my dear. I'll play with you. We are going to see who makes who beg," she stated defiantly.

"Okay Mommy," Kenneth readily agreed to Bella's challenge. He took the initiative right away. "You want to be a bad girl?" Yes I do damn it, Bella contemplated titillated by the moment. He spun her around, her back was to him. "Then I'm going to have to spank you. Bend forward Mommy and place your hands on the back of the couch for support." He leaned his body into hers grabbed her wrists and placed her hands just so. "Brace yourself Mommy." Bella's breath caught in her throat as she awaited the first smack. Kenneth landed the blow with precision. That was not his hand, Bella considered before she helplessly let out a little chuckle. "Oh so you think it's funny, hmm?" Kenneth asked. He made every effort to sound serous.

"Yeah, I really do." Bella continued to laugh. "As a matter of a fact, this is down right hilarious." She wiggled her ass playfully at him before stepping into character. "I'll be good. I can be a good girl. Really I can." Kenneth continued to whip her ass with his dick. "I won't misbehave again." Smack. Whack. "I promise."

"You know I don't like having to spank you but you've left me with no other choice so just stand there and take your punishment." Kenneth said, and the spanking continued. Bella pretended to cry. "Turn around," he demanded. "I'm go'n spank your pussy too."

"Oh no! Not my pussy!" Bella feigned fright. She attempted to run however Kenneth caught her quickly.

"Now see, I was going to go easy on you but you had to go and do that. Now sit your ass on the arm of that couch and open up your legs." Her compliance was immediate. "Spread your legs as wide as they can go, you naughty naughty girl." Again she obeyed. He whipped her clitoris with the head of his dick. Her pussy became wantonly lubricious, almost instantly. "You are a very bad girl," he chastised. The moist smacks turned into wet taps. Bella became extremely turned on by their little game. "Close your eyes Bella." She was in tuned with his rhythms, she anticipated every blow. Her breath deepened as her body prepared to orgasm again however just before she reached her climax he stopped. "Keep your eyes closed."

"Yes sir."

"Good girl."

There Bella was suspended in time, almost drowning in desire, as she awaited his next move. Her pussy pulsated, her vaginal muscles constricted and released greedily. She could barely breathe.

"Now I'm going to kiss everything inch of the flesh that I spanked."

Bella smiled at the irony of the situation and in that very moment reality seeped in: This man has called me Mommy since he was a little baby. He called his mother Mom. As he grew older he would always say, 'Mom is my mother but Bella is my Mommy because she takes care of me.' That statement has always touched my heart and now his tongue is touching my pussy. I have loved him since the first moment I held him in my arms and I love him still. He is my sweet baby. Oh my God what the hell am I doing? I can't do this. But damn it feels so good. Oooh wow, my, my, my… What's a girl to do? He has my cum all over his face. I really can't look at him as my little baby anymore. I know that he is a grown ass man but I helped raise him. I was there when he said his first word, took his first step, got and lost his first tooth, his first day at school, and his first date. This is wrong, so very very wrong. Ooh but his tongue feels so good on my pussy! Damn it all to hell! Ooooooh shiiiiiiit!

"Oh… Oh… M-mm… Oh… Aah… Oh… Sweet sweet baby. Mm-m! I'm going to cum! Oh! Damn! Fuck it! I want you! I need you to make love to me! Please! Please! Please! I want you Kenneth, you! Please fuck me…"

"You want me to fuck you?"

"Yes please."

"Me?"

"You Kenneth, I'm begging for your dick."

"You're so beautiful Mommy, just beautiful. Come with me, let me lay you down."

Kenneth stood up, took Bella by the hand, and led her over to the black velvet divan where she laid face down eyes closed. He began at her feet—he kissed every inch of her exposed flesh: he lingered on the backs of her knees, the tip of her tailbone, and the nape of her neck He turned her over and kissed his way back down again paying special attention to her eyelids, the tip of her nose, and every erogenous zone from her neck to her feet. He was gentle and very affectionate. Bella could feel the love he had for her in his every touch and in his every kiss. Kenneth parted her legs slowly as he crawled between them.

"I want you so badly right now Mommy."

"You can have me Baby. Take me Kenny… Please?"

Kenneth and Bella looked into each others eyes. He pressed the head of his dick past the outer lips of her pussy. He moved slowly, steadily, rhythmically, one centimeter at a time into the soft tight folds of her flesh. Bella's body lovingly welcomed him. Cum puddles formed on the black velvet coverlet. He pressed as gently as he could with each and every stroke until all twelve inches if his cock was glazed with her juices. He utterly filled the delta of her pussy. They paused for a moment—connected—one. There was no going back.

Bella closed her eyes for a moment. Her body helplessly quaked as the muscles of her vaginal floor gave way to spasm. Kenneth moved inside of her at an intensely sensuous pace. Flesh against flesh: hot, wet, and passionate. He increased his drive. She matched his velocity stroke for stroke. Eye to eye, nose to nose, lips to lips—Bella pumped her pelvis thrust after thrust—she met him half way and together, grinding in the middle, they strove to give as good as they got. A soft moan of pure ecstasy escaped her as her eyes began to lose focus and roll into the back of her head. Her lids closed.

"Look at me Mommy. Stay right here with me…"

"I'm here with you Baby," she said as she looked into his eyes once more, "trust me there's no other place my mind could be."

Kenneth and Bella moved together locked in a decadent dance created by their unique concupiscent rhythm. They held each other tight. Their continuous gesticulation was akin to sensuous tango. The perpetual erotic motion enveloped them—consumed them and before long they were lost in overwhelming emotion.

"I love you Mommy." Kenneth confessed.

"I love you too Baby." Bella could not help but to reciprocate. "This is so unexpected."

"Yes…" he sighed.

A tear escaped Bella's eyes just before she closed them again. Her love for Kenneth changed, matured. Little did she know that within seconds of the beginnings of her falling in love regret would rear its ugly head. *This is too much tenderness. I can't… Okay, we love each other but we are not in love and I won't allow myself to fall in love with him. What the hell is wrong with me? I've got to find a way to lighten up the mood. This should be fun. Sex should always be entertaining and exciting.* Bella opened her eyes and smiled up at Kenneth.

"Is this what I begged for Baby," she asked as she lifted an eyebrow, "I could've sworn with all that went on during your oral escapades you had some acrobats planned for the main act as well. Was I wrong?"

Kenneth did not miss a stroke as he spoke, "No Mommy, you were not wrong." He knew. She could hear it in his voice. "This is only the beginning. I have deep feelings for you Bella and I needed you to really know that and feel my love. This is the moment that we need to bond before we get down right freaky, because no matter how much I love you," Kenneth slowed his speech to match the stroke of his dick. "I'm going to tear… your… pussy… up! This is the calm before the storm my love."

"Oh damn…"

Kenneth's tongue rich kiss stirred pushed Bella to hedonistic abandon. He licked her neck and suckled her breasts hungrily. He ground his hips into hers, pressing deep and hard as he continued to speak. "Mm-m, Mommy, you don't know how long I've been waiting and wanting to do this."

"You know how freaky this whole mommy/baby thing is, right?" Bella added her own pelvic grind and pussy grip to the mix. They continued to fuck and talk. "This shit is kinky as hell!"

"Yes! It is my secret desire come true." He painstakingly moved the full length of his dick in and out of her pussy. He took his sweet time with each every pummel. "I was determined to have you."

"Really?" Bella smacked his ass. "Bad baby!"

"Oh, is it that kind of party Mommy?"

"Yes!"

"Oh okay," he replied, his smile devious. "Just remember you said that."

Was that a threat, Bella wondered.

Kenneth slid the shaft of his dick out of her pussy, leaving the head inside. Bella looked at him curiously as he knelt up, grabbed her ankles, and placed her feet on his brawny pecks. He lunged forward and gripped her hips. Her eyes widened in anticipation. He drove the full length his cock deep into her pussy. The splash of her juices splattered his chest and her cries of ecstasy penetrated the walls.

"The calm before the storm," Kenneth almost cooed.

"Bring the thunder baby," Bella challenged.

Kenneth rapidly power stroked Bella's pussy like well oiled pistons in a revved up engine. She dug her nails into his wrists all the while her body trembled under is energetic flow. She cried out his name in ecstasy as she came for him over and over again. Although he switched positions after every orgasm, like clock work, he never lost their connection. He placed her legs together, guided them over to one side and rotated her on his dick. He slapped her ass and he propelled his meaty cock even harder and faster. He inundated her body until her mind clouded, for her nothing else existed. Bella screamed through clinched teeth as she climaxed. Kenneth lay behind her, lifted her leg and tickled her clit while he continued pounding her pussy. Bella was reduced to taking tortured breaths.

"I'm cuuummmming!" Bella cried out unashamed.

"Stretch out your legs Mommy and roll with me," he instructed as his hand caressed her thigh. "Roll onto your stomach."

They rolled together. Kenneth kneeled up behind her with her legs between his, and gripped her ass and spread the cheeks. He slowed the pace to a leisurely grind which gave Bella time to catch her breath. She thoroughly enjoyed every inch of his cock. Her body quickened as her passions began to build again. Wave after wave of sensual gratification coursed through her body which pushed her higher and higher. She dug her nails into the sheets. Ever so slowly, Kenneth slid his dick in and out of her flesh. He took his sweet time yet again which drove her out of her mind. Bella was at his mercy. She wanted to buck back, to make him increase his tempo however he held her still. It was a sweet torture, orgasmic pressure leisurely rose from the deepest depths of her flesh and culminated and when her pleasure peeked, cum washed out like a tsunami, strong, violent, and all consuming. Kenneth rode it out like a master surfer navigating a tidal wave. It was the biggest orgasm Bella had ever experienced, after which, all she wanted to do was to bask for the duration, however Kenneth had other ideas. The few moments of post climactic bliss took place in the eye the storm. Kenneth gripped Bella's hips and pulled her towards him until she was up on her knees.

"Spread your legs Mommy put them on the outside of mine."

Bella obeyed eagerly. The moment she was in optimum position he tightened his grip on her hips and long stroked her pussy. He moved his dick inside of her from tip to base. Kenneth trusted his monolithic cock so deliberately that his balls slapped her clitoris with every plunge.

"Aaah! It hurt so good…" Bella cried out as a masochistic pang coursed through her heart and mind.

Footprints On The Headboard

Each thrust sent a boom cursing through every molecule of her body, like lightning striking through the clouds and touching ground. She bounced rearward on his dick until she came for him again. Bella's body purred so readily that it bewildered her.

"Sit back on this dick Mommy," Kenneth directed.

Pressed together they kneeled, her back against his chest, and moved as one. Kenneth caressed Bella's breasts as he pinched her nipples with one hand and spanked her pussy with the other. He hit her clit with each and every slap. He drove his dick briskly and with vigor. He overloaded her pussy and overwhelmed her senses with painful pleasure and raw passion. Bella thrashed fiercely as her mind spun: This is so intoxicating, yes, erotically deviant pleasures. The room is spinning, and my ears are ringing, sweet vertigo. I feel like I've been on a drunken binge for days. I need to cum again but I can't. Oh my gosh, I can't cum. Did I cum too much? Is that even possible?

There Bella was poised on the brink with her mind lost to conscious thought and her flesh spirited on by primal madness. Her body elongated as she struggled for breath. The need to cum overwhelmed all of her senses yet completion was denied her. Kenneth moved inside of her with purpose. His orgasm rocked his body with uncontrollable quivers and quakes. He let out a throaty guttural sound as he bucked. He painted her pussy walls white with his cum. His hot juices sent Bella over the edge one last time. She cried out as her liquid pleasure erupted and poured over his dick, and all over the chaise. They both fell limply onto its surface spent.

"Oh my god Mommy," Kenneth exclaimed breathlessly. "You are better than I ever dreamed."

"Thank you baby, you were so damn… Mm, my pussy feels fucking fantastic," Bella sighed. Kenneth smiled at her. They drifted off to sleep.

The beginning of next morning was filled with guilty grins and bashful glances yet no words. Kenneth made coffee while Bella showered. Bella made breakfast while Kenneth showered. The clink of fork to plate and the tick-tock of the wall clock were the only sounds that could be heard over the beating of their nervous hearts. After breakfast they relaxed on opposite ends of the couch in the living room with coffee.

"Thank you for last night Mommy, I really needed you." Kenneth said.

"Yes, you're welcome," Bella replied as she peeked over the rim of her cup. She savored a sip of Columbian coffee before she continued, "But you never told me why." She looked into Kenneth's eyes, and awaited his answer.

"Just before I got home from school my fiancé miscarried our child," Kenneth stated plainly.

"Your fiancé?" asked Bella as she smiled patiently.

"Yes. Her name is Daphne."

"Oh, okay. And um, why didn't you mention Miss Daphne yesterday?"

"I don't know. I'm sorry Mommy."

Bella closed her eyes for a moment. Her outward calm masked her inner thoughts and feelings: *What is it with people and their damn secrets? I tell the truth about my situation upfront but what do I get? I get confessions later on down the line, after all of the mind-blowing sex. All right young man, as we were.* When Bella looked at Kenneth again she had resumed her roll as Mommy, the woman who had always listened to him, never judged him, and always took his side right or wrong. She placed her cup on the table and opened her arms to him. Kenneth leaned in instinctively.

"Come here baby. Lay right here in my arms and let me hold you." Kenneth closed his eyes and wrapped his arms around Bella. She snuggled him in her bosom. "Okay Baby, tell Mommy what happened."

"I met her my junior year in college. We were lab partners and therefore we spent a lot of time together. For the first month we really took our time getting to know each other. I remembered what you said about most relationships breaking down within the first ninety days; how people's true personality finally begins to show by then. Well, one night, the night that we became lovers, she came to me crying. Her father had been killed in a car accident. She told me that she loved me and that life was too short not to express love when you find it. We had been together ever since. I asked her to marry me on New Years day of this year and she said yes. She told me that she was pregnant in March and I was so happy. I gathered her up in my arms and thanked her over and over again for loving me. That night we set a date. That date passed two days ago. Daphne lost our baby a week before the wedding and she walked out on me."

"Hush Baby, don't say any more. I'm so sorry you are hurting my darling."

Bella held Kenneth tight. She stroked his hair and kissed the top of his head as he cried silently in her arms.

"That's why I needed you so badly last night Mommy," he said as he looked up at Bella, his puffy red rimmed eyes begged for her understanding and pulled at her heartstrings. "I know you love me, you always have and you always will. I know that you will never just turn your back on me or leave me behind. But I didn't want you to love me as your surrogate son anymore. I needed you to love me as a man."

Ironically Bella smiled as she batted back her tears. She was at a loss for words, a growing condition which was aided by the fast developing lump in her throat. Kenneth's words touched and warmed her heart. They stayed as they were for a long while. Once he was all cried out he wanted to return the favor.

"Okay Mommy it's your turn." Kenneth said as he moved back to his side of the couch. "Come on I'll hold you. You can cry on my shoulder."

"I don't cry, at least not about that. It's just that," Bella sighed. "I can feel your pain, and it hurts my feelings to see you unhappy."

"You need to tell somebody about what's going on with you. Why not me? You know that I love you, and I'm here for you always."

"All right," Bella spoke in a very cold distant tone, one that was unfamiliar even to her. "I gave him everything that a husband could possibly want and need. I'm a good woman. I took my place in my marriage, happily. He was my king but he had no idea how to rule so I taught him. I ran the house, took care of his children, and he governed me. Our love life was wonderful. The only time I ever said no to sex was when I was menstruating and he allowed me that. Everyone knows how strong and willful I am but with him I yielded. He was my husband and I was his wife. We had ruff patches but my love for him never faltered. One day I came home from my book tour and he told me that he didn't love me anymore and hadn't for years. He further explained that he had impregnated another woman whom he had every intention of marrying. I stopped loving him in that very moment. It was as if the light in my heart simply clicked off. We spent Christmas, New Year's Eve, New Year's Day, and my birthday apart, a mutual choice. So the week after my birthday I slept with someone else. After all, I had spent all of that time being a loving faithful wife just so that I could have my fidelity thrown back in my face. Twenty years of loving the same man just to have it end like that was devastating. However Samson made me smile again."

"Is that the man that you're kind to?"

"Yes."

"Samson made my life exciting… Because we began while I was still married we always kept our relationship open. He lives in Europe now, military. We'd meet up in some place exotic a few times a year to play together."

"So why not get together with him?"

"It was never meant to be. He too is in love with someone else."

"Why is he still in your life?"

"Because he's a greedy selfish jackass," Bella laughed, half joking. "We get along well and we get over misunderstandings quickly. We care about each other."

"So, why does he make you so sad?"

"Because I have to let him go… I have to stand back and be his friend. I have to wish him well," she said with a sigh. "I don't want to."

"Can you?"

"Yes," she stated emphatically. "I like having him in my life, not just as the lover who helped me get past my broken marriage, I genuinely adore him."

"And there's no way that you two can be a couple—say to hell with what the world thinks and start a life together?"

"No Baby. That never was a consideration. As I said, we were lovers while I was married. He could never trust me to be true to him. Not only that, by the time I realized that I cared for him our relationship had already taken an acrimonious turn, but he still hung in there as my friend so I decided to become his friend too. As time passed I found myself thinking about him, wondering how he was doing, you know, just really missing him. My love for him is an easy love to bare, one that lasts a lifetime because it's unselfish. It's upsetting because I know that one day he will forget about me. He'll have his wife and his family and not need my love anymore. When we lived in the same city he would call me over just because he needed a hug. We always enjoyed each other's company no matter if we were lovers that day or just friends. But I haven't seen him in months."

"You are in love with him Bella."

"No I am not."

"Yes you are because you love him unconditionally. True love is selfless."

"When did you learn so much about love?"

"I learned it from you and then I shared it with Daphne."

"Well sweet baby, you are wrong about me being in love with him. There is a flaw in your theory."

"And what flaw is that?"

"I love you unconditionally. I have loved you since I held you in my arms for the very first time."

"That's a different kind of love and you know it."

"Touché," she said, "but know this, although I love easily enough, I have only been in love once in my life and that was with Mr. Howard.

"So Mommy, what are you going to do now?"

"I don't know. I've never allowed emotions rule my life and I sure as hell am not going to start now. I have always been duty bound, so really, there's nothing that needs to be done that can be done. I have to see my children through college which means no life altering relationships for a few more years. I'll wish Samson well. That doesn't change anything about my everyday life or who I choose to take as a lover. I'm thirty-seven years old, I don't have a period anymore, my children are grown, and I'm divorced so... I can do as I please."

"So can I be your lover while you are here? We can cheer each other up. Make each other happy, even if only for a little while."

"All right."

Bella stayed with Kenneth for almost a month. By the time she returned home to Phoenix she was ready to face her world.

CHAPTER THREE
HOME AGAIN

Bella was home alone and lost in thought as she relaxed in the tub, sipped red wine and listened to old school rap. Tupac's song, *Changes*, summed up her reality—the truth of her heart, and the convictions in her mind. Time passed unnoticed as she mused: I've made a lot of decisions about my future and I'm going to stick with them. Good God, how can everything in my love life change yet everything about my everyday life remained the same? So what, Samson is marrying someone else. I knew that day would come. I've made a lot of money writing about our escapades. Now I'm on to something new. I sit in safe and secure in my home unscathed by it all.

First things first I need to get this manuscript ready for submission. My life has taken an interesting turn during the Kenny-capades. I've learned something new about myself, I can be quite randy. Well, at least the St. Louis me was. The Arizona me is not. She's a good girl that got caught up in a bad man's game. None if this is my fault. If my husband wouldn't've cheated on me with an ugly woman I don't think I would've lost my mind like I did. I would not know Samson. I wouldn't have taken other lovers. I wouldn't have indulged in my ultimate freak-fest fantasies. Well, I'm all done with that. I'm home now. Nothing and no one can touch me here. I need to call Olivia.

"Bella!"

"Hey Olivia! I'm back!"

"Good! It's been boring as hell without you here. I have missed you so much. I can't even tell you how many times I went to call you to go somewhere with me but then I would remember that you were on the road."

"I've missed you too Olivia."

"Hey, what are you doing tonight?"

"Nothing girl."

"You want to meet at the pool hall for a beer?"

"Sure! I'm on my way!"

"Okay!"

Olivia was Bella's best friend in the world, the one woman who knew where all of her skeletons were buried. She was the type of person who would help dig the hole, throw the body in, and never speaks of it ever again. The ladies took a booth and ordered a round of drinks as they waited for a pool table to become available.

"Bella, you are looking good queen."

"Thank you," Bella said. "I have that picture."

"What picture?" Olivia asked, not quite following.

"Of young Kenny," Bella cooed.

"Let me see it," Olivia exclaimed.

"Here you are."

Olivia snatched the phone. She smiled as she studied every inch of photo. She looked at Bella and then back at the picture several times.

"Ooh Bella! I will say this… he is fine. How old is he?"

"Twenty-two," Bella replied bashfully.

"He looks it too."

"Take ten away from his age and you get his inches."

"Damn!"

"I know. He's far too young to have that much dick. But I will tell you this; after I get done with him he won't be making any mistakes with it ever again," said Bella brazenly although she thought: Not that he made any when he was fucking me. "He will be very well trained on what to do and how to do it." She continued. Not to say that he hasn't taught me a thing or two, she mused. "I'm going back in September."

"What about Samson?"

"He met someone, remember?" Bella asked nonchalantly. "I gained thirty pounds after that shit he pulled." She took a long draw of her drink as she waved her other hand dismissively. "It really doesn't matter. As you can see I've lost it and some. Young Kenny is good for me, and he can do the damn thing. I really don't want to have sex with Samson anymore. You have to understand how hard I came when Kenneth was fucking me. I haven't cum like that since I was in my twenties. I mean it gushed out of my body like ground water shooting from a busted pipe."

"Oh shit!"

"If I'm not loyal to anything else, I am loyal to good dick. I'm sure Samson will try to talk me into having sex again the moment his rose colored glasses fall off and he sees this fiancée of his in the clear light of day. But I'm not interested in him anymore. As a matter of a fact he doesn't even know I'm back. I don't think that I'm going to tell him either. I think it would be better to wait and see if we run into each other."

"How are you going to run into him?"

"He sent me an email telling me that he was moving back here. He's at Luke."

"That must be some damn good dick for you to do Samson like that."

"Sam has a lady love. Not only that I'm still mad at him for not having just a little faith in me last year. I don't care if he did apologize later, he should have just come and talked to me. He has always had his secrets remember when that woman showed up pregnant…?"

"Yeah, that was that bullshit."

"Yet he was able to top it all off with a secret engagement. Damn it! You have no idea how much that shit hurt me. He knows how my marriage ended."

"When was the last time you talked to him?"

"On his birthday, I called him from Dallas. Although he was happy to hear from me I rushed him off of the phone. I said that I didn't want to hold him up, I was just calling to wish him a happy birthday ok talk to you later goodbye."

"What?" Olivia asked shocked.

"What?" Bella asked indignant.

"You actually called him, wished him a happy birthday, and then jumped off the phone?"

"We're not connected anymore."

"What do you mean?"

"I asked him to say hello to his friend just before I hung up. He said he would however he sounded confused, so I asked him to tell me what friend I was talking about. Girl, he didn't have a clue. So I said the one that's attached to you. He still didn't know. So I told him to look straight down. That was when he laughed and told me that I wasn't right. Then I told him to always remember that that was what he always liked about me. I wished him a happy day and I said goodbye. We have always called our private parts our friends. It was our inside joke."

"And for the first time he didn't get it?"

"That's right. He's losing his playfulness, something I adored in him. He would always say naughty things like, "My friend needs to see your friend although he only has one eye." and I would say, "My friend likes your one-eyed friend she wants to give him a nice moist hug. You know she knows brail." and Samson would say, "Well you know that my friend can read lips." We were silly together. It was nice while it lasted."

"Don't you love him?"

"Yes, but I'm not in love with him. What does loving him have to do with my everyday life?"

"Absolutely nothing, if what you've told me about your Saint Louis vacation has any merit."

"I am not controlled by my emotions Olivia. I never have been. The most I've suffered can be summed up as being caught up in the moment. As you well know, I have never altered my everyday life for anyone since the end of my marriage."

"At least you have the common since not to put a man before your children. There are a lot of women who put their children on the back burner to pursue their own happiness. They go from man to man looking for love."

"I'm not looking for love. I just love to cum. I don't want to go from man to man, that's why I'm generally faithful to an excellent lover, well as faithful as I can be with men trying to play me like I'm stupid."

"So who would you say is the best?"

"Although my sweetness is shockingly good, my baby is the motha fuckin' bomb but even that didn't stop me from me from trying that young Jamaican."

"Jamaican?" asked Olivia choking on her drink. "What Jamaican?"

"Oh damn! That was supposed to be my little secret."

"Bella!" Olivia exclaimed still coughing.

"What?"

"Girrrrl!"

"Okay. His name was Omar. It happened on my last night of my twenty-eight day vacation to St. Louis a few months ago, not my last visit. My family threw me a bon voyage dinner. After dinner was over I called Kenneth. He was already in bed, at his mother's house. He offered for me to spend my last night with him, and of course I declined. I had to be on the road too early. I sat outside drinking and smoking with my cousin's neighbors as I often did on the nights that I was not with Kenneth. I talked to Omar almost daily from the beginning. He'd introduced himself the first day and asked if he could help with the groceries."

"Yes, your family loves your cooking."

"Indeed. Omar was six feet eight, with beautiful deep brown skin and a sexy accent. He had a nice chest, lovely brown eyes like pools of gold flaked chocolate, and a perfect smile. He flirted with me shamelessly, after the first week. I didn't think much of it until the time came to say goodbye. That night he took me by the hand and led me away from the group. We stood in the middle of a residential street, Saint Louis style, talking:"

"Bella, I want you. I cannot wait another day," Omar implored.

"Your wife is home."

Olivia interrupted, "His wife!"

"Yes, he married her for his green card. I met her, and she is a lovely lady who is doing a childhood friend a favor. She is openly gay and they both live separate lives. Okay! Can I get back to the story please?"

"I'm sorry, please continue," said Olivia taken aback.

"Okay now where was I? Oh yes… He took me by the hand and said, "Come to the park with me." We walked down the middle of the street together.

"What's at the park?" I asked.

"I have a special place I want to show you."

"Okay, I'll be right back," I said just as we were walking past my sister's house. "I'm going to go shower and change. I suggest that you do the same. I will not have sex with a dirty man."

When I returned he was at the foot of the steps waiting for me. I smiled at him, he smiled back at me. He took me by the hand once again as we walked to the park. He guided me to the middle of the park to a hidden French style gazebo with a picnic table surrounded by gigantic buckeye trees. The area, so densely covered by foliage, it was akin to a miniature forest. I would have never known such beauty was there had he not taken me. Judging by the way we walked we seemed to be in the center of a maze. The path was illuminated by the light of the full moon.

"Wow, Omar this is beautiful." said I. "It looks like something out of a fairytale, as if they made a gazebo out of Cinderella's carriage."

"This is my favorite place and I wanted to share it with you." Omar said before he kissed my cheek. "Let me take my shirt off for ya girl, so that you can sit down." Omar offered. He put his shirt on top of the picnic table. I took his stretched out hand as I stepped up on the bench and took a seat on top of the table. "That's better," he said as he stood before me. He slowly pushed my dress up. "Lay back baby and put ya feet up there withcha." He sat at the table as if he was sitting down for some Saint Louis style BBQ. "Yes, yes, that's it baby." He pulled me up to him as one would a dinner plate, bowed his head, and dove right in lips first.

"Omar," I gasped in delight. I stared up at the stars, and smoked my cigar as he ate my pussy. I felt so decadent puffing on my black and mild. He serviced me exceptionally well. His tongue swooped and swirled for a little while before he suckled my cum right out of me. My orgasm was hot and wet and he drank every drop.

"Can I have you now baby, my condom is in place," he asked after he gave my pussy one last juicy kiss. He stood up in such haste the bench was knocked away. He clamped his arms around my thighs and slid his rigid dick into my flesh like a hot poker piercing through ice.

"Yes," I cried out for the world to hear. "Give me some of that wild Jamaican lovin'." I commanded. "Omar… Omar… Omar!" Bella looked at Olivia and smiled devilishly. "Although he was not as endowed as Kenneth, oh my damn, his sex was shocking nonetheless. He fucked like a champion. Yes, yes, he was damn near mind blowing.

"What was it about him that fell short?" asked Olivia.

"He came too quickly. I still wanted to fuck."

"What happened after he was done?"

"We did it all again."

"Say what?"

"Oh yes."

"And you were smoking a cigar while he was…?"

"Yes as a matter of a fact I was. He was hittin' it from behind and I took a puff after every orgasm. He even said that it was unfair that he only came twice to my, he didn't know how many. I guess he has never been with a multi-orgasmic woman before. After all he was only twenty-four years old."

"What the hell has gotten into you?"

"I stopped dealing with men over thirty, which means as of the tenth of July Samson is too old for me."

"Good," Olivia said supportively. "I have a surprise for you."

"What?"

"Here he comes right now."

"Who?"

"Him, the youngsta right there."

Olivia pointed to a very attractive tall well built young man. He looked a little bit like Usher but with bigger muscles.

"Ooh yummy. How old is he?" asked Bella.

"Thirty, he is too old for you," said Olivia.

The ladies laughed together.

CHAPTER FOUR
THE SAGA

Bella had managed to maintain her friendship with Samson though they were not as close as they were before their trip to Spain. She did not feel the need to remain close to someone who would be so careless with her heart. Samson however refused to let her go. He knew she needed time therefore he communicated mostly by texts and chats and limited the regularity of his calls.

"Hello?" answered Bella absentmindedly.

"Hey pretty lady," Samson greeted a little too enthusiastically.

"Hello Sweetness."

"When did you get back?" he asked knowingly before thinking better of it, "or are you back yet?"

"I just got in two days ago," she answered easily all the while she thought: So you know I'm back? Cute.

"How was your trip?"

"Successful," she boasted. "I went to St. Louis, Atlanta, and Memphis, came back here for three days, and then I went up to Vegas and now I'm home again."

"Well it sounds like you have been doing a lot and having fun doing it."

"Yes I sure have. So, tell me Samson, what have you been up to?"

"Just chillin' with the kids and my girl, you know that there is not much to do here in Phoenix."

"So true, I thought about dating but I can't stand the thought of someone being in my everyday life. I have my children to consider, well that plus the fact that I like to come and go as I please."

"Well, why don't you come on over here?"

"All right…" Bella purred.

Bella showered and perfumed in a delicate Japanese cherry blossom scent. She dressed in a blue dress with matching pumps, that was all, no panties, no nylons, no bra. Samson greeted her at the door wearing nothing but his lovely smile.

"Hello Samson," Bella greeted as her gaze swept over his flesh. Humph, I see this isn't going to be a friendly visit, the prodigal lover returns, she thought.

"Good God Bella, you look hot! Come on in beautiful, come on in."

Trouble in paradise I see, Bella pondered as she attentively stepped past the threshold. She looked into Samson's eyes reached down and grabbed a handful of his cock. She unzipped her dress, and as she sashayed past him, she allowed it fall to the floor. He took pause, and watched her move. Bella pivoted and struck a daring pose for a moment. Samson locked the door. The second he turned to face her again she made her move, the distance between them closed swiftly as she leapt into the air mounting him. He caught her quickly, she secured her arms and legs tightly around his neck and torso.

"Fuck me Samson," Bella whispered heatedly. "I've missed you."

"And I have certainly missed everything about you." Samson said he hugged her tight. Of course you have, Bella thought, apparently amused. "Look at me," Samson said seriously. Bella straightened her face, and leaned back just enough to look into his eyes. "Forgive me Bella."

"Fuck me Samson," she said poker-faced. "Slide your pretty dick inside of my amazingly tight, hot wet pussy. And if you fuck me just right, maybe I will suck your dick later." He unceremoniously entered flesh with one magnificent thrust. "Oh yes…" Samson stood in the middle of the floor and fucked Bella until she trembled and her arms and legs fell away. He carried her to his bed and together they continued. "Let me taste you Samson."

Bella kissed and licked the head of Samson's cock and on down shaft. She twirled her tongue ring around and around working her way back up to the head again. She sucked his dick greedily. He grabbed a handful of her hair and thrust his cock deeper and deeper into her mouth, his dick snaked down her throat. His fervent moans spurred her on. She wanted to taste his cum however Samson had other ideas.

"I want all of you," he said passionately as he entered her pussy once more. "Ride Bella ride."

That should have been the beginning of the hottest sex they had ever had. Little did he know Bella was having second thoughts. As Bella looked into Samson's eyes her true feelings bubbled up to the surface of her mind and heart: I don't want this anymore. I never want to fuck him ever again. It is time to let him go. He has no idea that his wanting all of me today has changed everything, selfish bastard. All right lets get this over with.

"No trifecta for you," she said her voice light and sweet, "and you know why." Bella closed her eyes and concentrated solely on the sex act. Her mind spun: I needed to feel something else. I needed concupiscent desire, lascivious carnal passion, and sexual pleasure without all of the emotional bullshit. I needed to be fucked! I'll just ride his dick and not think pass my lust. Sex his ass like you have never done before. Make it very physical. Push him hard. Grind into him until you are too tired to move. Yes, that's it. Fuck him good. No matter how much time passes we will always be friends.

Bella fucked him as hard as she could however her emotions would not relent. She could not escape her thoughts… They needed to be drowned out.

"Take over Samson. I need to feel your power. I need you to fuck me hard, fuck my brains out," she demanded.

Samson pulled Bella down upon his chest and rolled with her into position. He placed her feet over his shoulders, gripped her hips, and fucked her hard. Ruled by desire, Samson's pace increased as his lust for her spun out of control. He scooped her up as he knelt back on his knees, gripped her hips and continued his sexual thrashing without missing a stroke. Bella held on for dear life and cried out in mindless unbridled sexual gratification. Samson switched positions several times. In the end, Bella was upside down over the side of the couch with his thumb in her ass fucking the hell out of her pussy.

"Tell me this pussy is mine," Samson demanded.

Bella rolled her eyes and she reflected: Oh damn… It must be worse than I thought over here in paradise. I'll just scream and moan and pretend I'm too far gone to respond.

On the drive home Bella tried to make sense of her interaction with Samson: Hot passionate sex with that man is always the bomb. Hell, I even got a few carpet burns to boot. What the hell was all that, this pussy's mine crap? I haven't seen him since Spain and when we talk its all buddy buddy. What the hell? Bella questioned as she rounded the corner and pressed the gas. Paul! His good buddy Paul saw me out having dinner yesterday. Oh that must be it! Paul waved and grinned knowingly, and of course he had no idea I was with dining my brother. He must have ran and told Sam that he saw me out with another man. Samson was making sure that he hasn't been replaced. He is not unhappy, he's selfish and I just got played, again. Well, I'm tired of that little game. It's time for me to make him take his place as a friend or leave me the fuck alone. I have to come up with a plan…

Bella mentally cursed Samson as she struggled to create a fitting strategy. She relaxed in lavender bath with a glass of brandy and fumed: Sam has got to stop playing with my emotions. He was the one who met someone and stayed out of contact for weeks Hell didn't bother to call me over until he thought I'd moved on as well. Samson needs to be taught a lesson and I know exactly how to teach him. He will definitely be out on the town this weekend; alas he has to stay away from his girlfriend for a couple of days if he doesn't want her to see the scratches on his ass and back and the nail prints on his wrists. My poor Sweetness has no idea what he's in for. Bella dried her hands and reached for the phone.

"Hello Mommy!" Kenneth answered right away.

"Hello! How's my baby doin'?"

"I'm not doing too well."

"Why baby? What's wrong?"

"I lost my job two days ago."

"Ooh Kenneth, I'm so sorry. Why didn't you tell me? I would have…"

"No Bella, I don't need you to do anything right now. I can make it."

"Okay if you say so. I won't push."

"Thank you."

"You're welcome. Hey Kenny, I've got a great idea," said Bella, as she thought: This couldn't have worked out more perfectly.

"What?" asked Kenneth.

"Come see me."

"When?"

"Tomorrow, damn it," Bella exclaimed cheerfully.

"What?" he asked astounded.

"I'll send you an e-ticket." Bella reached for her tablet. "Let me log on to see what flights are available."

"You really want me to come see you?"

"Yes, I'm lonely. I want to have some fun. You know how we do. I'll send you a limo."

"No need. I can call a cab. It'll be here by the time I'm packed. What do I need to pack? I know it's hot there in Phoenix. Can I wear jeans at night? How hot does it get anyway?"

"Don't worry about that. We'll go shopping for whatever."

"When is the next flight?"

"Wait a minute, you want to come tonight?"

"Hell yeah! I ain't got nothin' better to do."

"Oh, okay. There's a four-thirty flight, which you'll never make. The one after that is six o'clock. Then the last one is at seven-thirty."

"I've got frequent flyer miles. I'll be there as soon as I can."

"Eeee!" Bella squealed super excited. "This is going to be so much fun. See ya later baby, bye."

"Okay Mommy. I'll try to make the last flight."

"I can't wait to see you."

I'm so happy, my plan is going even better than expected! Now it's time to put the rest of it into action. Let me call the hotel that Samson's baby mama works at. Jenny is the best ghetto PR agent that money can buy. If anybody is go'n tell it, she'll definitely tell it all. She gets off work at six, so I have to get to the hotel before then to check in. The earliest Kenny could get here is around seven, perfect. Big mouth Jenny will see me check in but she won't know who my guest is. Okay, I have a few hours to kill so I'm going to go shopping. I need the bomb ass outfit for tonight, something tempting.

Bella had lost thirty pounds since Kenny and she became lovers and fifty pounds since she last saw Jenny. She happily shopped for the perfect weekend frocks. Bella chose a sheer white blouse that draped from her right shoulder over to her left hip and a pair of white Capri pants for the first night. She bought a pink outfit for Friday, red for Saturday and blue for Sunday, along with the matching purses and shoes. Bella finished shopping, packed her bags, and made a mad dash to the hotel. She arrived just before Jenny's shift ended.

"Hello, I have a reservation." Bella said her voice regal.

Jenny looked up, smiled briefly, and said, "Good evening, welcome." Her attitude was courteous yet dispassionate. She never really focused on Bella's face. She concentrated on the task at hand. "Your name please," she asked as she turned her attention to the computer.

She doesn't recognize me, Bella mused before replying, "Bella Howard."

Jenny's head snapped up. She frowned as she focused on Bella's face. It was Bella's turn to be aloof. She smiled patiently.

"Bella," Jenny asked baffled.

"Yes, Bella Howard," Bella confirmed amused. Jenny took a good look at Bella, a really good look. Bella pretend as if she did not know Jenny. "Is there a problem with my reservation," she asked narrowly containing her amusement.

Jenny stared, she was stuck. It was all Bella could do to keep her superior smile in place. Everything in her wanted to give into the laughter that was bubbling up inside of her. Jenny had not lost an ounce of fat since that baby was born. In fact she had gained a few more pounds. Jenny kept staring at Bella dumbfounded.

"What…" Bella asked, she blinked twice prettily and tilted her head to the left. "Do you want an autograph?" Bella smiled brightly.

That did it, Jenny finally snapped out of her reverie. Her shock was replaced by unmitigated hatred. Bella saw Jenny's ire however still she felt the need to push one more button. Bella pretended not to notice the change in Jenny's demeanor. Bella smiled even brighter as she whipped out a pen. She snatched up a hotel writing pad and then focused on Jenny's name tag.

"Who should I make this out to Jennifer or Jenny?" Bella looked boldly into Jenny's eyes and smiled her Hollywood smile as she awaited a response.

"I don't want your autograph Bella," Jenny relied seething.

"Oh my, excuse me. Are you fundamentally against romantic erotica?" she asked, her smirk accentuated her needling tone. "In any case you may call me Ms. Howard."

"Is that what Samson calls you?" Jenny snapped back.

"Do I know you?" Bella asked seemingly confused, although she thought: I'm go'n play this off for all that it's worth. I need to hold this look on my face for at least a full minute. One second, two seconds, three seconds, four seconds… Wow a minute is a long time… No, no, no, I can't laugh. I have to hold on to it a little while longer. Jenny is really pissed too! Forty-five seconds, forty-six seconds, forty-seven seconds… Close enough. "Jenny, hmm, and you know Sam… I take it you hold the title of baby mama. Now which baby's mama are you?" Bella teased. Jenny looked at Bella as if she wanted to slap the daylight out of her however all she could do was to stand there as Bella continued. "Oh, I know. You are little Tyron's mother? Oh my… it really is you?!"

"Yeah it's me," Jenny retorted hostilely.

"It's been a while. Now that I think about it you haven't changed a bit, other than a little weight gain. I should have recognized you right off the bat but I meet so many people on my book tours. Tell me how's little Tyron doing?" Bella thoroughly enjoyed aggravating Jenny, so much so she babbled on. "Only one of your sons belongs to Sam, right? I remember now. You had a child by your husband first but he left you, then there was Sam but he left you too. Then there was the fling with your best friend's man but she kept her man however they both stopped talking to you. Did your husband come back or are you divorced now? This could make a great story line." Bella paused, regained focus, and asked, "Did you find my reservation?"

The look on Jenny's face said so many vile things Bella was shocked. She expected a look of 'bitch' but if looks could maim and kill Bella would have been dead and disfigured, dental record identification kind of mutilation. Bella knew damn well she was being callus and hurtful however she really did not care. She wanted to hurt Jenny, and therefore she did. Jenny was so angry Bella could feel the hate vibes billowing out of her very soul.

"Hello," Bella sang, "my reservation? Should I ask for a manager?"

"One moment," Jenny turned her attention back to the computer. She focused so hard on the computer screen that one would have thought she had forgotten how to read English all together. She finally spoke, her voice was cold and distant, "The penthouse suite for you and a guest?"

"Yes," Bella continued to croon.

"You may leave your guest's name with the front desk. He or she can pick up the key upon arrival. All they have to do is show an ID."

"No thank you, I'll take both keys." Nice try, thought Bella.

"I show that your reservation is from Thursday to Sunday." Jenny returned to professional mode. "Check out is at noon. The hotel offers complementary limo service to and from the airport. Breakfast is served from…"

Bella half-heartedly listened to Jenny's spiel as she continued plotting: I'm pretty sure Jenny is going to tell Samson but I have to be certain. I have to find a way to let her know that I still see her baby daddy sexually however the man that's shackin' up with me this weekend is not him. Oh I know, she said something about a limo. That's the ticket. But how do I get Samson back into the conversation? I'll think of something. Let me interrupt her.

"You said something about limo service?"

"Yes but it's only to and from the airport."

"Perfect. My guest is coming in tonight. What are the hours?"

"They're available two hours before the first flight and an hour after the last flight seven days a week, with a reservation or at least two hour prior notice."

"It's six our time, eight his, so he must be on the seven-thirty flight. I have just enough time if he lands at eight-thirty. Do I make that reservation with you or what?" Before Jenny could answer Bella's cell phone rang. "Just a moment I have to get this." Bella stepped away from the reception desk. "Hello Baby, did you miss your flight?"

"No, I just made my connection in Albuquerque." Kenneth replied his voice a little stressed. "I'll be in Phoenix in about an hour."

"What? An hour," Bella asked a little bit too excited.

"Yes Mommy I made it to the airport in time to take the four-thirty flight. I'll meet you in baggage claim."

"I didn't think you'd be able to make that one. When you land go to the south curb, I'm on my way."

"Okay."

Bella returned to the check-in counter. "Jenny I don't need the limo after all. Are we all done here? I have to get to the airport posthaste."

"No not quite."

"Can you hurry it along please? All I have to do is sign something and get the room keys right?"

"I need to see your credit card."

"Okay, just a sec." Bella rifled around in her purse. "Here you are, the credit card with which I reserved the room." Jenny took the card and went back to working on the computer for a moment longer. Bella waited not so patiently, her mind racing: I'm going to go ahead and get out my driver's license too. If I'm right she'll ask for it the moment I put my purse back on my shoulder. I'll just put it in my pocked just in case. So, you want to take your time do you? Jenny finished her game of Family Feud looked up and smiled. As soon as she did Bella reached into her pocket.

"And your driver's license?"

"Yes, I thought you just might need that." Bella stated in the most condescending tone that she could muster. She handed over her license. "How long have you been doing this?"

Jenny did not respond with words. She paused just long enough to share a dirty look, after which she continued processing the reservation.

"I need you to sign here."

"All right."

"Here are your room keys."

"Thank you."

"I take it you don't want me to tell Samson that I've seen you?"

"You may tell him whatever you want to tell him. He didn't believe you before so why would he believe you now?"

"Oh, so you still keep in touch with him even thought you are rich and famous now? You don't need him."

"I never needed him darlin'. I want him in my life and he wants me to be in his. We're really good friends, really-really good." Bella smiled her innuendo. "Why would that ever change?"

"I never really believed that you two were just friends. I still think there's more."

"Why? Because I didn't give birth to his baby, I don't buy him things, and I don't give him money, yet he still comes around—I'm still in the picture?"

"I know it has to be more than just friendship. You're far too cocky. You always have been."

"Smart girl…" Bella said with bravo, after which she smiled dazzlingly, and turned to walk away.

"He has a new girlfriend," Jenny yelled out before Bella could get two feet away.

Bella stopped, she did not turn to face Jenny as she spoke, "You can't beat me at this game Jennifer," warned Bella, her tone calm yet menacing. "I like hurting you," Bella stated audaciously. "Do you really want to get your feelings hurt, again?" She stood her ground for a moment longer before she walked out of the hotel. Bella stopped at the limo stand. The driver looked bored to tears. She smiled her brightest smile and greeted him, "Hi!"

"Yes ma'am?"

"Busy?"

"Nope, I have nothing else scheduled until ten o'clock tonight."

"Can ya take me to the airport?" She showed him her hotel key card as she casually slid him a fifty.

"Right away ma'am," he agreed with a smile. "Champagne?"

"Why thank you."

Once all settled in and on her way, Bella's mind could not help but to go back to her moments with Jenny: She has not changed one bit: her attitude, the unhealthy attachment she has to Samson, and the bitter hatred she has for me. Everything about her is exactly the same as it was over five years ago. I should have told her that I was just at Samson's house, that I just left his bed a few hours ago. I could have told her that his having a girlfriend didn't stop him from fucking me today. I should have told her that if three baby mamas and a fiancée, which are all his exes now, could not stop me, what kind of hope did a little girlfriend have? I could have told her that Samson will never let me go, that I'm his and he is mine no matter whom no matter what!

Ooh she got to you. No she didn't! Oh yes Bella, she did. Anytime you start thinking about what you could have said to her or how the conversations should have went; you know damn well she got under your skin. She'll pay for that when I'm her baby's stepmother. Awe, see, now you've gone and jumped off the deep end. The last thing you need in your life right now or ever is a husband with baby mamas, plural. You've already been married and divorced. You've done a great job raising your children. Marriage? To Samson? You, a stepmother? Really? Awe, hell naw! I would be punishing myself more than any other person on earth. What I need is a playmate. My sweet sexy young Kenneth is exactly what I need. But I'm still go'n get her ass.

CHAPTER FIVE
DOING TOO MUCH

Bella relaxed in the back of the limo and contemplated the need for psychotropic medication. She laughed and toasted the highlights of her day. Just as she was pouring her third glass of champagne young Kenneth called.

"Hello baby," Bella greeted lovingly.

"Hey Mommy," Kenneth replied, his spirits lifted. "Where are you?"

"I'm in the hotel's limo. I'll be there in a few minutes. Where are you?"

"I just got through baggage claim. I'm in line to get a cup of coffee."

"Good you are going to need it. I'll be the black lady dressed in white standing in front of the burgundy limo," Bella said happily. "Hey, get a cup for me too and then come on outside. I want…"

"I know what you look like Bella," Kenneth said with a laugh. "And I know what you want.

"Okay just remember what I said."

Minutes later the limo parked curbside at passenger pickup. Bella spotted Kenneth exiting the south curb door fifty-two caring his suitcase and a cup holder with two coffees. Bella jumped out of the limo yelling his name. He stopped and looked in her direction however he did not move towards her.

"Kenny," Bella yelled again, "black woman, white outfit, burgundy limo!"

"Bella?" Kenneth asked not quite believing his eyes.

"Yes it's me!"

"Wow," he said before he eagerly made his way to her. Bella smiled and bounced a little bit as she waited for him to get close enough to touch. "Daaaamn girl!"

"I know right," Bella beamed.

Their eyes locked and filled with the joy of their hearts from one lover to the other. Bella opened her arms. Her hands greedily beckoned him to her. Kenneth freed his hands as he passed the limo driver all in one fluid motion. He gathered her up into his arms and wrapped her legs around his torso. They held on tight for the longest moment. Bella's mind went aflutter: Fuck Samson! I've got my baby right here. Mm-m, this is going to be good! I have a plan to get even with Samson but if it doesn't work I'll still have my Kenneth. The trick is not letting Kenny know what I'm up to. The driver opened the door and cleared his cleared his throat.

"Hello Mommy," Kenneth said, he loosened his grip.

"Hello Baby," Bella replied as she stepped out of his arms.

"Being single really agrees with you Bella."

"Thank you." She kissed his cheek. "Baby, I'm so sorry you had to run into such bad luck."

"Thank you Bella. I'm glad you called me."

"Mm," Bella smiled as she thought: The only time Kenneth calls me Bella is when he is being serious, to emphasize his point, or when he is making it clear that we are on the same adult level. "It looks like my timing was perfect Kenneth, let's go."

"More perfect than you know Mommy." Bella and Kenneth settled into the limo where a fresh glass of champagne and a box of chocolates awaited. "Is all of this for me?"

"No. It's for me." Bella smiled smugly. She popped a chocolate into her mouth. "Yum, do you have any prospects?"

"Yes, I have a headhunter who is hard at work on that front." Kenneth smiled appreciatively. He placed his hand on her knee and looked into her eyes longingly.

"That's good," said Bella casually. "Are you seeing anyone special?"

"No, but I did see my ex." Kenneth said before he took pause. Bella failed to react and therefore he continued, "Daphne gave me back my ring. She said that she needed her mother and her family. She said that she never got over loosing our child and the fact that we are broken up made it worse but she has learned to live without me." He took a deep breath. "Bella, she was the one who said that we shouldn't be together, not me."

"I'm sorry Kenny."

"She claims that she flew all the way to St. Louis to tell me to my face how she doesn't want nothin' to do with me. She handed me the ring and a box of things that reminded her of us and bounced."

"Oh baby…"

"She told me that she never wanted to see me again..."

"Stop!" Bella interrupted. She gently lifted Kenneth's hand from her knee and lovingly kissed his palm. "You are here with me now. I'm going to take your mind off all of that nastiness. I know you're a good man with a loving heart. Daphne wasn't the one for you or she wouldn't have hurt you like that. You'll find the perfect woman one day. Until then, I am here for you as your lover, your friend, and your mommy."

"Thank you Bella," he said. He hugged her tight.

"You should've called when she first showed up on your door step."

"I know."

"Finish your coffee. After we get unpacked we are going to happy hour."

"Kiss me Mommy."

Just as the kiss ended the limo door swung open. Bella and Kenneth walked through the lobby to the elevator, where he grabbed her from behind and kissed the sweet spot at the nape of her neck. In a moment of lightheartedness she threw caution to the wind and laughed a bit too loudly. Little did she know that Jenny volunteered for overtime just so she might catch a glimpse of Bella's guest.

Kenneth pinched Bella's nipple playfully. "Ouch!" she cried out and swatted his hand. "Bad baby! Stop that."

"I have missed you Mommy. I can hardly wait to get you naked."

Bella's gaiety secured the unexpected attention of her rival. Although caught off guard by the angry pair of imposing eyes that stared calculatingly into hers, Bella did not alter her behavior. Jenny stood there taking it all in as if she was attending her first picture show, which made Bella laugh even more. Kenneth added to the scene with a slap to Bella's derrière as the elevator doors opened. Nestled in Kenneth's arms, Bella's eyes found Jenny's. Take it all in bitch. Run to Samson and tell him all that you have seen tonight. This is the bonus that I would have paid top dollar for. I couldn't have planned it any better, Bella mused sadistically. The elevator doors closed.

Once their luggage was brought up Kenneth showered and changed for cocktails. Bella and Kenneth passed through the lobby on the way to the hotel's bar. Bella caught site of Jenny once more. I cannot believe it, there she is working, still. I guess she wasn't waiting on a ride. Please don't tell me that this woman picked up a second shift just to spy on me. Okay, so I have a spy. We are leaving for the club at nine. I have a little under two hours to crawl under her skin and I'm gonna do just that too. All I have to do is get young Kenny a little bit tipsy and he'll do the rest. Let her watch me being wanted by a sexy young man.

Lulled by revenge Bella quickly forgot that Kenneth had not eaten that evening. She was abruptly reminded an hour later as he was drunk, horny, and all hands. What began as a well choreographed enchanting seduction suddenly turned into something completely out of control and vulgar. Before she knew what was happening Bella was snatched up and dragged out of the bar. As they waited for the elevator Kenneth's need, fueled by copious amounts of liquor, became more than a little bit suggestive. His words were down right raunchy and his actions were sexually explicit, displayed for all to hear and see.

Kenneth pressed Bella up against the wall like one of those, cowboy and blond hooker scenes fitted with naughty whispers and juicy kisses to her face. Bella giggled like a school girl under Jenny's watchful eye. Once the elevator doors opened Kenneth entered backwards pulling Bella in along with him. When the doors closed what only could have been described as the remnants of his habitations, were quickly swept away.

"Why don't you ever wear skirts Mommy?"

"My pants zip in the back."

Kenneth dropped to his knees and unzipped Bella's pants as he went. He burrowed his head between her legs and nibbled her pussy through her thong as far as her zipper would allow.

"Turn around Bella and brace yourself." He instructed and she acceded. He pulled her pants down, snapped the bottom string of her g-string and snaked his tongue into her pussy. He feverishly licked her flesh from behind until the elevator bell rang signaling their floor. Before the elevator doors opened he stood up, and zipped her pants as he went. After which he turned and exited first. Bella smoothed her shirt and her hair, and followed him into their suite. "Bella, take everything off except for your shoes and then turn and face the wall," Kenneth commanded the moment Bella entered the room.

"Yes my dear…" Bella complied expeditiously. Fully dressed Kenneth dropped to his knees once more but this time as he slowly began to stand, he took her with him. He forced her to climb the wall like spider woman, until he stood straight up with his face buried in her ass until she came. A river of her pleasure ran down his face. Kenneth kissed Bella's butt cheeks, spine, and neck as she slid down the wall little by little. The moment her feet touched the floor he took her right where she stood. He fucked her salacious pussy, like a twelve inch hot knife slicing through butter. Bella cried out. "Kenneth! Oh please!"

Bella's mind spun. Not today! I can't take this! Not today! I've got to get him to stop. This is truly too much for me to take, way too much. Oooh, I forgot how enormous his dick is. Damn! How drunk was I? How did I take his dick? Oh shit! Breathe Bella, maybe if you cum it will take some of the pain away. I think I'm going to faint. What the fuck was I thinking? I was drunk everyday for weeks in St. Louis dealing with this man. Oh sweet Jesus, I remember now. I saw it and wanted to try it but even then I knew I was too short to fuck with him however, I was inebriated enough to be fearless. If my memory serves me right, he has longevity to boot. I can't! Oh God I'm going to cum. Oh shit the pain is fucking with my pleasure. Combine them Bella, be brave. Damn it man!

"Kenneth… Kenneth," All she could do was cry out his name and gasp urgently for air.

"Hush Bella," he whispered insistently. "Hush, be strong."

How the fuck am I supposed to be quiet? I know I'm wrong for fucking both Kenneth and Samson in the same day but it couldn't be helped. My body was primed and ripe for the picking and my heart was filled with revenge. But this shit hurts like hell. I've cum three times already. I really can't take this. Please stop! Oh please, oh please, oh please, this is too much for me! I'm losing control. I have never said stop ever before in my life but I have to say it.

"Stop!" Bella hit the wall and screamed out like her sanity depended on it.

"Stop?"

"Please!"

"What?" Kenneth did not stop but he did let up a bit. "You can't take me?"

"That's not it!" Bella lied. She closed her eyes and though: Yes it is. Your dick is too big. "I didn't see you put on your raincoat."

"You don't have to worry," Kenneth said his stroke still gentle. "I put it on."

"Let me see!"

"Look straight down."

He showed her quickly. Kenneth stroked straight through Bella's thighs and then back inside of her pussy all without missing a beat. Oh damn, Bella thought. He is definitely condom clad. This is some S & M type shit for sure. His dick is my pleasure and my pain, one agonizing orgasm after another. What the fuck am I supposed to do? How can I make him stop? Oh my God, oh my God, oh my God.

Bella's wits spun out of control all the while she searched her mind for an escape. Every orgasm pushed her closer and closer to the edge. Although she struggled to concentrate, she slowly slipped into a sadomasochistic abyss. Bella struggled to breathe. She gasped for air yet her breath caught in her throat. She could not swallow. The added struggle gave her a way out.

Her mind cleared just long enough to say, "I need a drink!" Bella said between pants. "I'm so thirsty. I've cum way too many times."

"Now?"

"Yes now." Bella's voice cracked as she spoke. "I've have cum over and over again darling, I'm parched. See the puddle on the floor? I need a drink then we can continue with this in the bedroom. After all we have never had sex in an actual bed before."

The moment Kenneth slid his rigid cock out of Bella's delta her knees buckled. She steadied herself against the wall for the briefest of moments before she made a mad dash to the mini bar. She poured a triple Jack and quickly drank it down.

"No I guess we haven't…" Kenneth replied as he eyed her curiously. He knew something was wrong, and he wondered, was it him? "I just see you, I want you, and I take you. That bar looks sturdy."

"Oh no you don't!" Bella said momentarily halting his approach. She poured another triple. "Take that old condom off. I bought a box of XLs. It's in the room on the dresser."

"Just hold on to the bar for a few minutes," Kenneth suggested. He grabbed a hold of Bella. "I'll go easy on you until you adjust to me again and I brought plenty of condoms. We can take it nice and slow," he continued as he entered her once more. "Drink your drink and let me take care of the rest."

"Ooh yes," Bella cooed. She closed her eyes and basked: That's more like it, mm, very nice indeed. Now this I remember, an extremely fulfilling pleasure evoking stroke. Why was he trying to kill my pussy earlier? This is divine, oh yes… yes yes yes. Let me squeeze his dick tight, ah, I'm cuming.

"Yeah Mommy, I love that little thing you do. Your pussy is so tight."

"Mm-hmm! I'm cuming again baby," said Bella as pleasure washed over her.

"You feel so good to me Mommy. Yes that's it, cum for me," Kenneth encouraged. "I love the way you cum Mommy."

"Let's take this to the bedroom Baby, and I'll show you how good that little trick can really be. I might even show you a new trick or two. I've got some skills baby."

"Show me Mommy," he agreed passionately. "We go'n put some footprints on the headboard."

Bella giggled, finished her drink, and headed for the bedroom with young Kenneth in tow. The liquor warmed her belly as it made its way through her blood stream. Her inhibitions were long gone and her pussy was ready for more of what Kenneth had to offer. Bella stopped just outside of the bedroom door. Her hand rested on the knob as she turned to Kenneth.

"Before we get started what was with all that up against the wall stuff?"

"What? Didn't you like it?"

"Yes and no."

"What?"

"I liked it in the beginning climbing the wall was erotic as hell, sliding down was the bomb too, but actually being on the wall well, it got to be too much."

"It was too much for you?" he asked in disbelief.

"Well yeah! There was nothing to hold on to. I was busy trying to stay sane: clawing the wall, balancing my pussy on your tongue all the while worrying about my safety as I reacted to sexual pleasure. Do you know how out of control I felt trying to balance myself and cum too?" Bella smiled nervously before she continued, "And the way you fucked me afterwards… I couldn't believe you were so much to take. I mean I remember what your penis looks like and what your sex feels like. I know damn well you have a monolithic dick but I really didn't think that you would try to tickle my heart with the tip of it."

"I was not trying to hurt you Bella. You are a lot smaller and tighter than you use to be. You kept cumming so I thought you like it. I didn't know I was killing your pussy until you screamed stop." Kenneth smiled sheepishly. "I made an adjustment."

"I did like that wall crawling thing," Bella admitted bashfully.

"I know," Kenneth said perceptively.

"I'm sorry. Come on into the bedroom with me and let me show you just how much I enjoy the way you fuck me baby."

"You ain't said nothin' but a word."

"Get in the bed, lay on your back, and lie very still." Bella instructed. "I have a special treat for you. Relax and close your eyes."

The fact that Kenneth was so young gave her a great advantage. Bella enjoyed the thought of being that older woman he talks about for the rest of his life. In her hearts of hearts she only wanted his happiness and their shared pleasure.

"Okay Bella, I'm ready," he said eagerly. He wiggled his derrière and grinned.

"Are you now?"

Bella's heart was set on reciprocity. She had to pay young Kenneth back a little bit for the wonderful way he made her climb the wall. She was prepared to use a lot of skill and a few choice techniques. She considered it very necessary for some reason. Bella watched Kenneth lie as still as he could, however he did not stay still for long. Bella relaxed on her belly between his legs. She massaged his balls and stroked his dick until it was soaking wet from tip to base. She placed her thumbs on the edge of his pubic hairline and licked the ultra-sensitive spot right beneath his scrotum. Kenneth helplessly moaned her name and spread his legs for more. She gently pressed his perineum, the spot where her tongue played, as she moved forward.

"Bella…?"

"Trust me baby," she shushed.

Bella methodically licked Kenneth's flesh from the base of his balls to the tip of his penis over and over again until he cried out and writhed beneath her. She paused just long enough to smile victoriously all the while maintaining the light pressure on his perineum. Consumed by uninhibited sexual pleasure, Kenneth trembled and panted and roared. Bella pressed on, he was her ice cream, her delight. She crawled up on her knees, placed her thumbs on the erogenous zones at the edge of his public area and continued on from the base of his balls to the tip of his dick: left, center, right, center, again and again. Kenneth cried out like a wounded animal and bucked uncontrollably as the pleasure of orgasm washed over him.

"My God woman," said Kenneth mystified. "I have never…"

"I know," Bella interrupted, her sexually charged egomaniacal tone and smile spurred him on.

"Come here girl," his lusty demand thrilled her.

Bella and Kenneth, intertwined in an oral smorgasbord, tasted, sampled, and drank each other's juices. Somewhere along the way, their sex game became serious. An extremely fundamental element of what they shared suddenly changed. They fucked like jungle animals on the Serengeti—primal and all consuming yet carnal hunger gave way to epic intimacy, as they got caught up in a whirlwind of desire and the steamy satisfaction of making love, shared feelings that would change everything between them forever. When it was all over he held her close.

"Bella," Kenneth took a calming breath and continued. "It would be so easy to fall in love with you."

"Oh Kenny," Bella began. Although she felt the same way about him too, she was not so quick to verbalize the secrets of her heart. "I um…"

"Look at me Bella." Kenneth all but demanded. Bella sat up and faced him. He took her by the hand, looked into her eyes, and took yet another deep breath. "Bella, I really do care about you."

"Baby, that's the best part about being a lifelong friend," she interjected, desperately not wanting to hear any confessions of romantic love. "We can love, care for, and protect each other as much as we want and still wish each other well."

"I don't want to wish you well. I want you all to myself."

Oh shit, Bella thought, and yet she said, "Kenneth, you're rebounding. We should leave things the way they are for now. If you still feel the same way in ninety days come tell me. I really don't want things to get all weird between us." She closed her eyes and covered her face with her hands. Her mind helplessly went back to the last person who hurt her poor little delicate feelings: I lived through that already with Samson. He thought he was in love with me but as soon as he figured out that he wasn't he acted weird. It almost ended our friendship.

"I know how I feel."

Bella uncovered her face, looked intensely into Kenneth eyes and said, "I know better than you…"

"What do you think you know about my feelings that I don't know? What do you see that I'm not seeing?"

"Look, I know there are things that you love about me. I selflessly share with you and care for you so you love me for it…"

"What do you mean by that?" he asked almost hostilely.

"Well, first of all, I'm not talking about money. You've loved me your whole life. Adding sex to that love just might have clouded your judgment a little bit," said Bella with a condescending little kiss to which Kenneth scoured playfully. "Anyway what I meant to say was I openly share myself with you. It is so easy for me with you and you with me because we love overtly. I love you so without hesitation or reservation because you are the only person who has never hurt me. You're open and honest about what you are going through. I had a friendship before, when I was going through my divorce. I was open and honest but he wasn't so we never grew as close. I can honestly say I don't ever want you to be out of my life. But that doesn't mean you're in love."

"I love you Bella," he said sincerely.

"I love you too Kenneth." Bella smiled egotistically and said, "How can you not love a woman like me? I have a brilliant yet sexy mind, an exquisite face, a hot body and a sweet tight juicy pussy."

"And an ego out of this world," he said and laughed.

"My sense of self is healthy. The problem is, you are used to women who undervalue themselves." Bella paused briefly. "Listen, I want us to love one another through thick or thin until the end. I want us to be able to wish each other well if or when we ever finally find the one. I want us to care enough about the other person's feelings to be a homey when one of us is dating someone else, a lover when the mood strikes, and the trusted friend we confide in through it all. I'm here for you baby but I cannot be your one and only."

Kenneth stared at Bella. He searched her face for clues to her true feelings, cracks in her armor; however Bella's poker face revealed absolutely nothing despite the fact that she thought: I really do love you Kenny, but I unwillingly love someone else too. Thank God you don't live here although I'm so very happy you're here because I need you right now. Too bad you're eleven and a half years younger than me. Too bad I let Samson under my skin, although it might be nice to have you both.

"Why not?" asked Kenneth baffled.

"You're not ready for that. You're still in love with your ex-fiancé. I'll help you through it as your lover and your mommy. But once you're all better you won't need me. You'll be free to date and we'll still have each other, mommy and baby. We have loved one another for far too long for either of us to ruin it all by trying for a romantic relationship now."

"It sounds like I'm using you."

"Really, you're not. Using me for what exactly? You're here just because I said I was lonely. You've never asked me for a damn thing. You've never shown me anything but love and respect. Now why would we mess this up with relationship crap?" Bella took pause: Oh my God! I'm one of those women who fell for the man that doesn't quite treat her right. Damn you Samson!

"All I'm saying is keep an open mind Bella."

"Okay I will. Come on baby lets get showered and changed. We've got some partying to do."

Bella and Kenneth were dressed to dance and party the night away. By the time they returned to the lobby of the hotel little Miss Jenny was no longer manning the reception desk. But damn if she wasn't one of the first people they ran into at the club. Bella pretended not to see her as Kenneth and she made their way to the bar. Little did they know as they moved on to the Soul Food Kitchen window, they were being watched by someone else. Kenneth waited for two whiting dinners while Bella scouted for a table. She felt lucky to find one although it was right up front by the dance floor. Before she could get comfortable in her seat friends and fans gathered, greeted, and congratulated her, which Bella enjoyed. Kenneth and Bella drank, ate, dance, and had an all around good time. After a couple of hours Kenneth excused himself to the men's room. As soon as his back was turned Samson made his moved. He walked up to Bella drink in hand.

"Hello pretty lady," Samson greeted Bella as if the situation was perfectly normal.

"Hello Sweetness," Bella replied in kind.

"So, who are you here with?"

"My friend Kenneth."

"Your friend?" he asked suspiciously.

"Yes, my friend. Are you here alone or are you with the lady in your life?"

"I came out with the fellas."

"Oh okay. Well, my friend should be back any minute. Would you like to meet him?"

"Are you two dating?" he interrogated.

"No, I thought about dating but like I told you earlier, I just can't wrap my mind around someone being in my everyday life. You know me, I like to do what I want to do when I want to do it, no questions asked."

"What… is he what you want to do?" he questioned hostility apparent.

"You have a girlfriend Sweetness, you can't possibly be jealous," she said as she smiled up at him shrewdly.

Samson took pause for a moment. When he spoke again his timbre had returned to normal, "What are you drinking tonight?"

"Jack."

"Here." He placed the drink on the table and walked away.

Bella was more amused by Samson's display than perplexed. She watched as he disappeared into the crowd. She giggled as she thought: I didn't even get the chance to thank him for the drink. Seconds later Kenneth sat down next to her.

"Who was that?"

"Samson."

"That's Samson?" Kenneth asked unimpressed.

"Yes."

"Really?"

"Um-hmm. What…?" Bella asked confused.

"Nothin'." Kenneth said as he leaned back in his chair and smiled.

Kenneth looked like he didn't have a care in the world, as if Samson wasn't shit. Bella liked it. Her mind was filled with happy thoughts: My baby is the perfect homey lover friend. I think I'm going to have to keep him and suck his dick tonight.

CHAPTER SIX
A NIGHT TO REMEMBER

"Come dance with me Bella," Samson asked out of the blue. There he was, standing boldly in front of her. She excused myself, took his hand, and followed him out to the middle of the dance floor where Samson acted badly. He danced like a hip-hop star making a porn video fully dressed. Bella felt as if she had to find a way to talk to him, alone. But before she could figure it all out he took her by the hand and led her out of the club.

"Where did you park?" asked Samson the moment his foot hit the pavement.

"I didn't drive," Bella replied with calm curiosity.

"Well I did. Come on."

Samson still had her by the hand as he basically dragged her behind him through the parking lot. Bella wore four inch heals and she really did not feel like walking over the rough cracked asphalt to his car.

"That limo is mine," she said as they approached.

"Is it open?"

"Yes."

"Get in," he demanded.

"Okay," she agreed. The driver opened the door. Samson lost most of his reason to jealousy. He looked at Bella, with blatant hostility. The look he gave her clear said: That ain't the man you came with. She shook her head in total disbelief. Her next words cleared things up for Samson a bit, "Thank you. We are not leaving."

"Yes ma'am."

As soon as the door closed Samson started in on her, "Weren't you just at my house this afternoon?"

"Yes."

"And tonight you are out with him?"

"Yes."

"So what is he to you?"

"My friend."

"Um-hmm, your friend."

"Don't you basically live with someone? I mean her picture is up on the wall in your bedroom."

"She has nothing to do with us."

"He has nothing to do with us."

"Where did he come from?"

"What do you mean?"

"I know he ain't from here."

"He came in from St. Louis a few hours ago."

"From St. Louis?"

"Yes."

"So, how long have you known this friend from The Lou?"

"Over twenty years."

"What? How old is he?"

"Twenty-two or three."

"So you've known him since he was what, two?"

"Something like that, I used to baby-sit him. In fact he has been my baby since he was just a weeks old."

"Oh damn! Ain't that a bitch?"

"Looky here Sam, I can't live my life waiting on you to remember me. There is no way in hell I'm going to go for up to six months without having sex either. It's just not going to happen. Hell, six weeks is pushing it. I always have time for you no matter what no matter who, just as we always promised each other but can you say the same to me?"

"Bella…"

"I'm not done. You are looking for what I've already had therefore I have a certain level of understanding. Moreover, there hasn't been a woman that you've been involved with that you've been faithful to since you met me, so if you marry one of them you are making a mistake and you know it but you keep them around because of what they do for you."

"Oh so you telling me that you ain't doin' nothing' for ole boy?"

"When I ran into him I was flat broke. I was staying with my sister in St. Louis and driving my mama's car. It was his first summer home from college. To this day he has not seen my house or my car. When I saw him again a few years later, I told him that I got a book deal, and again to this day, he hasn't asked me for shit."

"Give him time," Samson said bitterly. "I've never asked you for shit either. I paid for everything when were together. Ain't no other woman ever got like that but you."

"You ain't right. What is it Sam? What's the problem? I can't have any friends other than you? I can't finally move on now that you've met someone? How many girlfriends have you had over the years? It's my turn to have someone."

"Didn't you say you didn't want anyone in your everyday life?"

"Yes. He lives in St. Louis."

"Is he my replacement?"

"No Sweetness, no one can replace you, but you met someone. I'm alone. You left me alone in Spain months ago. I felt lonely today so I asked him to come see me. You just so happened to call me a few hours before he arrived. What did you expect me to do?"

"You gotta do what you gotta do. I ain't mad atcha," he lied. "I know you have to get yours."

"Let's go back in. We are being rude."

"I wouldn't wanna keep you."

Bella turned away from Samson and thought: Ooh he mad. I just hope this doesn't backfire. She exited the limo and headed for the club. Samson stopped at the door.

"What's wrong Sweetness?" she asked as she looked up over her shoulder into his eyes.

"When is he leaving?"

"Sunday."

"Good."

Bella faced forward and smiled deviously her mind raced: Yep he's mad all right. He definitely doesn't want me with anyone else. It was okay when I lived my ex-husband, because he never saw anyone out with me. It was as if no other man existed. Now that I think about it he has never seen me with anyone else until today. When Bella returned to her table Kenneth was out on the dance floor.

"There's your friend," Samson was all too happy to point out.

"I see him," Bella said with a shrug.

The minute Kenneth saw her sitting at the table he joined her.

"Where did you go?"

"Out to the limo."

"He still cares about you Bella."

"No he doesn't. He's like a child and I'm the toy that he doesn't want anyone else playing with. Let's change the subject. You need another drink?"

"Naw, I'm straight."

"Bullshit! Drink up! We came out to party and have a good time. After all we have a limo, the perfect designated driver."

Bella ordered bottle service and challenged Kenneth to keep up. He had forgotten that she could drink him under the table, and she was counting on him passing out that night. She needed him to be three sheets to the wind and by the time they left and he was. He could barely walk straight. As a matter of a fact as soon as he got into the limo he passed out still talking about what a good time he had. At the hotel Bella had to get help from the limo driver to get Kenneth to the room. No sooner than she got herself settled in, there was a knock at her door. Who the hell could be knocking on the door at this hour? Maybe we left something in the back of the car. Did I forget to tip the driver? No. I'll bet that Kenny's wallet fell out or something, she pondered as she strolled across the room to the door.

Bella opened the door talking. "Hi, did we leave somethi…" her voice trailed off as her mind took control: No the fuck he didn't. Calm down Bella. You can't let him know that he surprised you.

"Come on in Sam. I thought you were the limo driver."

"Where's your friend?"

"Kenneth is in the adjoining room, one of the perks of having a suite."

"What, you're not sharing a bed?"

"No."

"That's right, you like to sleep alone."

"Who is your girlfriend sleeping with tonight?"

"You really do want to start some shit tonight, don't you?"

"Nope, I was just asking. Since I'm asking questions, why are you here?"

"I came to get you."

"Excuse me?"

"You heard me."

"It's almost three o'clock in the morning. Shouldn't you be asleep? Don't you have to go to work tomorrow?"

"If you get dressed and come on home with me, I can get in a couple hours of sleep."

"Come on," she said as she took him by the hand.

"Where are we going?"

"My room… If we are going to be scandalous then we might as well go all the way with it. If you are going to be bold enough to come here then I'm going to be bold enough to let you stay here."

"We're staying here?"

"Sure why not. What time do you have to be up in the morning?"

"Six, why?"

"I'll call down for a wake up call. Come on let's go to bed, I'm tired."

Samson happily climbed into her bed. Of course he had to get some pussy before drifting off to sleep. Bella laid there staring at the ceiling, wide awake, lost in thought. *Oh sweet Jesus, I cannot believe this is actually happening. I think I've bitten off more than I can chew. How am I going to deal with the two of them all weekend long? This is worse than when I was married. At lease back then I could pick a fight with my husband so that I didn't have to give him any sex. I actually like both of these men, no scratch that, I love them both but in different ways. How can I get out of this weekend turning into a fuck fest?*

Needlessly to say, Bella could not find a way to say no to either man all weekend long and it goes without saying, she enjoyed every lusty detail about that weekend. No matter how she looked at both men thrilled her, and therefore she acquiesced. The debauchery began again the next morning with a wakeup call.

"Wake up Sweetness," Bella said. Samson was dog tired and dragging his ass. He absolutely didn't want to move. She got up and started the shower. She jumped in first thinking that he would join her, but when she returned to the room he was fast asleep. She slapped his ass. He finally got up. "Get in the shower. I'll make some coffee."

Bella dressed and left the room. She tiptoed over to Kenneth's room, peeped in and saw that he was still dead to the world. She went to the kitchen and started the coffee. When she returned to her room Samson was in the shower. She picked up his clothes and stuffed them in a hotel dry cleaning bag, straightened out the bed a little bit, and laid on top of the covers. The next thing she knew Samson was sitting next to her.

"Bella, I don't have anything to wear."

She got up and took off her t-shirt and shorts and handed them to him. "Here, I'm coming to your house to get them if you don't bring them back today."

"They're mine!"

"No they're not. You gave them to me almost two years ago. I wear them when I don't feel like getting dressed. Please don't make me come get them."

"What time is it?"

"Six-thirty."

"I don't have time for coffee baabay. I've gotta go. Walk me out."

"Just a sec, let me get dressed."

"Where did you put my clothes?"

"Right there in that bag."

Bella threw on a sun dress, slipped into some strappy sandals and followed Samson out. Now at that point in time Bella had no idea Samson was setting up a coup. The moment the elevators opened she realized she'd been had. Jenny glanced up just as they stepped out. Samson's arm snaked around Bella's waist. All she could do was smile as she appreciated the truth of the matter: Samson would not have known where to find me if Jenny had not told him. Bella surmised by his actions that whatever Jenny said to him must have derogatory. Samson focused all of his attention on Bella as he guided her to the front door. He took her into his arms, grabbed two hands full of her ass and kissed goodbye before he left.

"Bye Samson," said Bella. I might as well add a little bit of fuel to the fire, she though as she ginned deviously. Let me go on over there and ask Miss Jenny a question, Bella thought as she strutted to the reservation desk smiling all the way. "Good morning," Bella greeted coolly. Jenny seethed as she glared at Bella's smiling face. If she could have gotten away with murder, she would have already hopped over the counter and choked Bella to death, still Bella smiled. "What time did you say breakfast is served?"

"Breakfast is served from six to nine Monday thru Friday and from seven to ten on Saturdays. Champagne brunch is served on Sundays from nine to noon."

"Thank you." Bella turned and walked away. She had not gotten three steps away from the reception desk when she heard a Jenny mumble bitch under her breath. Although she kept on walking Bella had to make one thing abundantly clear and therefore she said simply and calmly, "Don't get yourself fired." However, her mind kept going a moment longer: You're the help Jennifer, here to serve me and disrespect will not be tolerated.

About two hours later Kenneth and Bella came down for breakfast. They smiled at each other and held hands on the elevator. Jenny spotted Bella and Kenneth immediately after the elevator door opened however Bella's attention was fixed on getting one more kiss. Once Bella saw the look total shock and disbelief on Jenny's face she almost hit the floor laughing. The hilarity of the situation, even with Bella's strongest effort, shined threw her normally impenetrable poker face. Bella sashayed by glanced over at Jenny and laughed out loud. She knew it was wrong of her but she just could not help herself.

"What's so funny?" asked Kenneth.

"I'll tell you over breakfast."

Once they were settled in with a plate of food and some coffee Kenneth asked again, "What was so funny earlier?"

"My nemesis works here."

"Who?"

"I'll show you after breakfast."

"But why is that funny?"

"I was involved with her youngest child's father."

"What's so funny about that?"

"She hates me for it and the look she gave me as we walked by made me laugh. We were about the same size before I lost the weight." Bella took a sip of coffee and shrugged. She continued to smile as she surmised: Or it could have been the fact that there is only one way in and out of the penthouse suites, and both of you came down with me at different times this morning. She is pretty sure that both of you spent the night in my suite last night. The question is: Who did I have sex with or maybe I fucked you both. God help me if anybody knew the truth, especially seeing as young men wake up horny. Ooh wee my pussy has been busy. If this is any indication of how my weekend is going to go, I need to exercise my pussy every free moment I have to keep her tight, starting now. "It's a girl thing."

"Who? Ole girl that looked like the ogre's wife, Fiona?"

"Oh no," Bella gave in, she laughed until she cried. "No you didn't say Fiona?"

"There's a difference you know," said Kenneth with a smile. "Bella you are beautiful it doesn't matter how much you weight or what size you are. I've never seen you not look absolutely stunning. On the other hand she looks like a big ole yellow ogre. If she had a bangin' body most men would not mind her face looking like that."

"Yeah, I saw pictures of her when she was smaller."

"What, it should have been a hit it and quit it kind of thing but she got pregnant?"

"Yep, that about sums it up," she said still laughing.

"Who, your friend from last night?"

"How did you guess?"

"When we got here yesterday she gave me a dirty look."

"So, do you still see him?"

"When I'm out and about, but he has a girlfriend. He informed me that it was serious just after our trip to Spain, remember? I heard through the grapevine they were talking about marriage. As a matter of a fact I had not heard for him in weeks, until yesterday."

"He acted like y'all were still together."

"He did didn't he? Poor boo-boo."

"What did he say to you in the limo?"

"He wanted to know who you are, how long you are staying, and what kind of friend you are to me."

"What did you say?"

"I said that you are my friend from St. Louis, you are staying until Sunday, and you are a friend who has every benefit possible."

"You told him that we get down?"

"Yes. What? Was that supposed to be a secret?"

"Naw… I'm just saying."

"As long as he has a girlfriend I have every right to see whom ever I want."

"So what happens to me if they break up?"

"Nothing, if I'm not free when he is, he has to respect that just like I've respected his relationships. We have a friendship that will stand the test of time if neither one of us gets jealous or possessive or hateful. I can't see a problem."

"So your relationship with him is just like your relationship with me?"

"No. I have loved you almost all of your life and even if one of us did get mad or jealous so what. We'd eventually get over it. Nothing and no one can separate us. There's no question about that."

"What if he wants more from you than a friendship and occasional sex?"

"Well, if a man wants more from me, he had better make himself very clear from the get go. The way we start is the way it will always be. So don't ask for a lover when you are really looking for a wife." Bella took a sip of coffee. "But it's not solely up to what a man wants. I have to want him as well I would have to be open to change. I'm divorced, I have just signed a three book deal with a New York publisher, I have endorsements, and my children are impressionable young ladies who are attending college. Now is not a good time for the confines of a romantic relationship."

"Sometimes you have to make it a good time. Sometimes you just have to go for it."

"I did go for it. I was with my husband for over 20 years, remember? I'm concentrating on my girls' education and my career. I really don't have the time or the patience for someone to be in my everyday life. I don't want to hurt anybody by being neglectful and I don't want to be hurt by anyone vying to get back at me either."

"I understand, but what if the person is trying to find their own way but they know in their heart that they want you to be the one that they share the rest of their life with, then what?"

"What?"

"Say the person wants to finish grad school but they have to work their way through so they have a regular forty hour a week job plus school."

"Um-hmm."

"With studying and work, they won't be taking up a lot of your time."

"What if that person and I grow apart during the time we are both trying to find our way in life?"

"I don't think that will happen but if it did, through it all, you and that person would always remain friends."

"How can you be sure that someone wouldn't get hurt? You know how it is when someone gets their feelings hurt. It's very different than jealousy or anger. With a broken heart, hate grows, and then you never want to see that person ever again."

"With a friendship like ours I could never hate you. If we try and fail then we'll have to live with that regardless of whose fault it is."

"You don't sound hypothetical anymore."

"I know."

"Let's just see how this weekend goes."

"Take it slow? I can do that."

"Let's talk about you. I thought you were buying a house."

"I was looking at a few properties but it doesn't look like I'm going to be able to do that."

"Why not?"

"Between my family nickel'n and dime'n me and loosing my job I'm doing good just to eat everyday."

"Did you apply for unemployment?"

"Oh yes, that same day."

"What do you have in savings?"

"My down payment, closing costs, and two mortgage payments."

"Okay. Let's finish eating so we can go site seeing downtown, after that we will have lunch, and after lunch we can go shopping, and then I'll take you up on South Mountain where we can go horse back riding at sunset and have dinner. Its Friday night, we can go club hopping later on tonight if you'd like. I reserved a limo for every night starting at nine. We can drink all we want."

"What do you normally do on a Friday?"

"I lay around the house until about three, watching the soaps and movies. When I get up I take a shower, do my hair, get my outfit ready, and go to happy hour. If I have no plans to go out, I work."

"That sounds good to me."

"What do you mean?"

"Let's hang out Bella. I'm not trying to get into your pockets."

"The horse back ride is only twenty dollars."

"Okay, and what were we going to go shopping for?"

"Just incase you forgot something."

"I didn't forget anything. There's nothing that I need, except for you."

"Okay then."

"Don't get me wrong I love the fact that you want to share with me but that's not who we are. We didn't start off that way and I don't want it to turn into that kind of relationship. Why are we staying in a hotel anyway?"

"I thought it would be fun. We have a Jacuzzi in our room, room service, pool, massage, and maid service."

"Don't you have everything at your house except for room service and massage service?"

"Yes, but my maid only comes three times a week, and my Jacuzzi is outside."

"I don't need this swanky hotel thang, although we will be trying out that Jacuzzi later on today."

"You're so nasty," Bella said suggestively.

"Let's go!"

It never took much to get Kenneth going. He snatched Bella up by the hand, swept her off of her feet, and carted her off to the room. She giggled the whole way. Meanwhile Jenny ogled, her heart filled with envy and hate. The one thing that was very consistent about Kenneth was when he wanted to have sex with Bella he never cared where they were. He'd find some privacy some where. She liked that about him. He cradled her in his arms as he stood in front of the elevator. He gazed at her in-between kisses while we waited for the doors to open. Suddenly Kenneth put Bella down. She stood before him confused however her confusion gave way to laughter when he did his stretches and licked his lips greedily. He gawked hungrily at her as if she was his next meal which made her feel like the sexiest woman in the world.

My baby, my sweet Kenneth is so much fun. I love his desire for me, the way he openly shows how he feels, his longevity and his cockiness. He treats me like I'm his, not just my pussy. He treats me like he can't get enough of me. He calls, he e-mails, and he sends card, candy and flowers. Now that I think about it, he treats me a hell of a lot better than Samson ever did. Do I really want Samson or am I feeling possessive because his current girlfriend has lasted so long? Bella lost her train of thought the moment the elevator doors opened. They stepped in, alone.

"Wrap your legs around me." Kenneth instructed.

"Why?"

"Because you are wearing that sexy little sundress and I have been trying to be good since you slipped it on, but now, I have run out of will power."

As he spoke he put on his condom, Bella watched. She wrapped her arms around his neck, jumped up and clamped her legs around his waist. She smiled in appreciation and kissed his neck. She leaned back and looked into his eyes.

"I'm so excited baby, I want you too. I want you so much right now, no one else matters," Bella declared.

Her eyes rolled up and slowly closed as she felt Kenneth's dick enter her flesh. He spun around and pressed Bella's back against the elevator wall. She grabbed onto the railing for support. He fucked with maddening zeal. Kenneth was completely exhilarating. The elevator was only the beginning. He didn't stop just because the door opened. Bella thanked God the coast was clear. She did not quite understand how he got the door open all the while driving his dick in and out of her pussy but he managed. He pumped his hips as he carried her over to the back of the couch. "Lie back Bella," he said after he positioned her on top of the sofa back. Melodious vibrations began deep inside of her pussy and rushed through her body as her blood rushed to her head. Enthralled by orgasmic bliss, all she could do was feel and thoroughly enjoy the moment. Bella needed a shower and nap when it was all over. Kenneth helped Bella in the shower.

"We go'n have to fuck in here before we leave," Kenneth stated, his St. Louis accent very pronounced.

"You are so very, very, very bad." She looked into his eyes and smiled. "Insatiable. I'm going to be that older woman that you talk to your sons and grandsons about, that wild ass woman that you got to do thangs with."

Kenneth laughed and said, "Turn around Bella, let me finish washing you so I can put you to bed."

"I need a back rub too, please," she asked sweetly. Bella turned her back to Kenneth, bowed her head, and mused: I am tired though. Fucking them both as been more than just a little bit challenging…

"I know. You didn't have to ask."

"Why thank ya baby."

"I'm here for you for as long as you need me to be."

Is that because you really care for me or because you lost your job? No Bella, don't even think that. He wanted you and was down for you when you didn't have nothin'. Even if he is needing you right now, a little bit more than he is wanting you, so what. Just keep your heart out of it so that when it's all over you can still keep your friendship. After all that is a whole lot of pleasure giving dick to have to give up, not to mention his energy level and stamina. Ooh and his freaky, fuck at the drop of a hat, mannerism. He is definitely a keeper.

CHAPTER SEVEN
TIMING IS EVERYTHING

Kenneth sat on the foot of the bed and watched Bella sleep. When she opened her eyes he was the first thing she saw.

"Why are you looking at me?" she asked curiously.

"You were talking in your sleep. I thought you were calling out to me so I came in to see what you wanted."

"How long was I talking? Better yet, what did I say?"

"You were talking for about five minutes. You were talking about me, about us."

"What about us?"

"You wanted to know if I was for real." He climbed into bed behind her and took her into his arms. "You said you didn't want to get hurt again. You told me that you didn't want to jump into anything so soon after getting your divorce. You went on and on about it not being enough time, which means that when we were together last year you were still married."

"Technically I was, but we were living in two different houses, I had filed for divorce over a year before I got with you, and my default application was already submitted. Not even thirty days later the divorce was final. When I came to see you in September I was single," she said as she snuggled in his arms.

"It doesn't even matter at this point."

"Would it have mattered then?" she asked.

"Truth be told, no. I wanted you then just like I want you now."

"How do you feel about your ex-fiancée?"

"Why do you want to talk about her at his particular moment?"

"I need to know."

"I use to think that I loved her until I fell in love with you."

Bella stared at Kenneth like he had grown two more heads instantly. She could not say a word for the longest moment. She was completely dumbfounded. She got up and walked away.

"I have to use the bathroom." Bella said as she exited the room.

"I'll be right here when you get back Bella."

Kenneth sat up in the bed and waited for Bella. He stretched out his arms to her to rejoin him when she returned. She happily climbed back into bed and snuggled into his embrace. He held her tight.

"I found a job on the internet while you were sleeping," he said proudly. "I called them. I have an interview set up for Monday. It starts off at fifteen dollars an hour, with my experience and after ninety days, it goes up from there depending on my job performance."

"So you are going to move here to Arizona?"

"Sure, why not? I found an apartment that lets you pay by the week. All I have to do is save for a few months and move into a better place."

"You worked all this out in an hour and a half?"

"Yeah, I'm a man on a mission. When you called me yesterday I was low. You always seem to be there exactly when I need you, from the day we met to today. I want to be there for you too. I still can't believe we got together. I know we can make it work."

"Well damn! You know what Kenneth, I'm going to have to play wait and see."

"I expect that from a show me state girl."

"Good. You know that I love you too, but I'm not in love with you Kenneth, at least not yet. I will not risk getting hurt. You are making it too easy for me to fall for you. That shit scares me to death. If you break my heart I would really hate you then I would have to cut you," Bella ended half joking.

He laughed, "Come on girl."

"Where are we going?"

"To the Jacuzzi."

"I'm too old to keep up with you and your ravenous sex drive."

"That's why you smile every time it's time, right?" he asked as he wiggled his eyebrows. "I know I excite you. You know if you want me before I say something to you, you can come my way, right? Make the first move I'm always ready for you."

"Oh really now?"

"Come on over here Mommy and let me show you."

As Bella snuggled close to Kenneth her mind went adrift: I have no idea where all of this emotion came from. I couldn't admit my own feelings to myself but to him it came out of my mouth without preamble. I love you, good God I do love him. I'm in love with Kenneth the man, not the memory of the sweet love I had for the little boy as I first believed.

Bella's mind drifted while they made love in the hot tub: Here I am with my with the young man who I use to baby-sit telling me he is in love with me and he's moving to town because he wants a future with me. It's amazing how much can be covered in a total of two minutes—a two minute conversation followed by some hot steamy sex. There should have been a full blown three day discussion about Kenneth moving to town… to be with me… in my everyday life… as my one and only lover… exclusively… but nope, it was all covered in just two minutes. Oh my lawdy, I'm coming. He has such a lovely dick.

Bella did not remember to think past the moments she shared with Kenneth until she was getting out of the shower, for the third time: I have got to get the hell out of this suite. I need to talk to him without lust interrupting my train of thought. I have to be able to think clearly. How the hell am I going to talk him out of his plan? There is no way in hell I can handle Kenneth and Samson living in the same city or state for that matter. First Samson moves back here from Europe and now Kenneth is moving here from St. Louis… What the fuck is that? What time is it anyway?

Bella checked her phone it was just before two in the afternoon. Good heavens, I'm still all tuckered out. I need some time to myself and my pussy needs to recuperate, he-he-he. I need to get some more sleep or I won't be able to party later on tonight. Bella called down to the spa, she desperately hoped they had an opening. She walked into Kenneth's bedroom dressed in her robe. He was sitting on the bed tying his shoes.

"Baby," Bella greeted.

"What are you up to Bella?" Kenned asked as he reached up and pulled her down onto his lap.

"Well, I scheduled a spa treatment for you. You get a massage, manicure, and pedicure. Your appointment is at two."

"That's in five minutes."

"The spa is only an elevator's ride away."

"Aren't you coming too?"

"No. I'm exhausted. You'll be gone for about two hours and in that time I'm going to nap a little more. I didn't sleep well last night."

"Why didn't you come climb in bed with me last night?"

Because Samson was here, she reflected guiltily yet said, "Because you would have kept me up all night." Just like Samson did and I would have had to sleep with ice on my swollen pussy like I do now. "Go, I need to add to the whopping three hours of sleep I got last night." I wonder how much weight I've lost in the past twenty-four hours. Who needs a zumba when there's fucking? "Go on. Enjoy," Bella concluded sweetly.

Bella relaxed across the bed happily alone. She stretched out on her belly and cuddled a pillow. The moment she drifted off her cell phone rang. She reluctantly picked up the phone and looked at the call screen and immediately thought: Oh damn... What does Sam want now? I just want some fucking sleep.

"Hello Sweetness," Bella answered as cheerfully as she could.

"Hello there pretty lady. You sound tired." Samson said worried.

"You didn't let me get much sleep last night," she said, and then thought: And young Kenny has been wearing me out all damn morning and afternoon.

"The elevator won't go up to your floor."

"You need a key. Where are you now?"

"Just under you," he said his tone dripping with innuendo.

"You are here in the hotel?"

"Yeah."

"Please be kidding," she said exasperated.

Samson busted out laughing. When he sobered he said, "I'm still at work baabay. I'd like to talk to you if you're not too busy."

"What's on your mind?"

"You. Can you meet me later on today?"

"I really don't think so, seeing as I have company."

"What are you doin' now?"

"I'm lying down right now. I'm trying to take a nap."

"Where's ole boy?"

"He is down stairs getting a massage."

"So you are up in the room alone?"

"Yes."

"I can be there in fifteen minutes."

Bella laughed, she could not help but to. It took her a long time to flip the script on Samson. She was the one always trying to fit their little liaison into his schedule. She stopped dating because he said that he wanted her all to himself. After their trip to Jamaica, Bella's feelings for Samson confused her heart and mind. Confusion gave way to the pain and frustration as she laid on the beach in Spain. Samson had met someone. He was the one in the relationship and she the one who was free as a bird and flapping her wings. Finally, she thought, things have changed. Bella rolled onto her back, put her phone on speaker and placed it between her breasts. She tucked her hands behind her head smugly.

"Sweetness, why are you coming after me now?"

"I just realized that you could actually get away."

"What?"

"When I met you, you were married. I knew you weren't going anywhere. After your divorce you got the book deal. I knew you needed time to concentrate on your career. I figured you didn't have time to start any new relationships when we began living out our ultimate freak-fest fantasies in some of the most beautiful places in the world."

"So, because I have a friend, you have to stake your claim. Remember, you met someone. A few months later I was in Belize all alone thinking and drinking… You never showed."

"I paid for your room and your flight," Samson said defensively.

"It was supposed to be our… Never mind. What about Savanna?" Bella asked calculatingly. "She loves you. She has put up with your cheating, your baby mamas, and she pretty much lives at your apartment. Are you really going to hurt her like that?"

"I just want to…"

"Keep your place in line?"

"No Bella." Samson replied the anger clear in his voice.

"What then?"

"I still what to be your 'no matter what, no matter who' Bella."

"Who said that that has changed? The only difference now is I'm super single, super fit, and enjoying every minute of it. I'm not alone anymore. As a matter of a fact this is the first time you've ever seen me with someone else isn't it? Besides the one time that you saw me out with my husband, the night we met."

"Well, now that I think about it…"

"Quit bullshitting me man. Don't trip."

"I'm not trippin'," he said defensively.

"You trippin'! The only time I fucked anyone else was when I was on vacation or on tour. You were semi-okay as long as it was some meaningless tryst but that didn't last long. You asked me to be exclusively yours but that didn't last long either because, out of the blue you told me that you met someone. You've made your choice Samson which freed me up to make a few choices of my own. Remember you are the one who abandoned me."

"Abandoned you?"

"Yes, I enjoyed our vacation alone in Belize thank you, and you haven't planned a damn thing since." Bella took a calming breath before she continued, "When I was on tour I invited you to meet up with me a few times but you never came, Kenneth did. I always invited you first but after the third time you turned me down I stopped inviting you. I figured that the relationship with your girlfriend was really serious; it had to be your love for her. You chose her over me time and time again."

"So what, now it is time for you to do the same to me?"

"No, I've never chosen anyone over you. All of the other choices I've made have always been secondary, plan B. I had no idea that you were going to magically reappear in my life this weekend after all you've been back in the U.S. for months. What's the deal with that anyway? Why now?"

"I haven't heard from you in a while. You reach out to me once a month to check up on how I'm doing and to tell me what you have been up to but I haven't heard from you since March."

"I would have called you for your birthday in July."

"Are we reduced to birthdays and holidays now?"

No Sweetness, never that she thought yet she said, "What can you offer me? Can you be faithful to me and trust me to be faithful to you as I gallivant across the country and around the world doing book signings at male strip shows and sex workshops? You hate my Erotica and Eye Candy tour. Can you live without the monetary perks that your little girlfriend sends your way every month? Because you know I ain't giving you shit."

"Let me call you back," said Samson abruptly.

"Okay," she agreed with a click that ended the call immediately.

It's time for me to rethink this whole thing. I don't want a traditional relationship with Samson or Kenneth. Damn it, I'm no better that Sam. All right, think… I've always been the one both men could always rely on therefore I need to come up with a plan to see who is really serious and who is just trying to make sure that I don't go no where. It's a hard thing to figure out even though I have known Kenneth practically all of his life, everything changed the minute we became lovers but Samson's story is a little bit different. He has never allowed me to drift too far away from him. It didn't matter what we were going through independently, he has always made sure I was still a part of his life. Well, after this weekend I'll know the truth, I hope.

The main problem with Kenneth is the fact that his first love and unborn baby was recently taken away from him. He's hurt. He just might be holding on to me for comfort. I can let him do that without risking getting hurt, I think. The major problem with Samson is his baggage, I'm not sure I want to deal with his children's mothers for the next fifteen years or so. Samson and Kenneth are far too young for me although they're both excellent lovers. My sexy Samson and my beautiful big dick Kenneth... I could keep them both if I can just keep Kenneth out of my state, Bella mused just before she drifted off to sleep.

Little did she know that young Kenneth would awaken her an hour later with delectable oral pleasures. She woke up in the throws of full orgasmic bliss. She gripped the back of his head and pressed his face deeper into her delta as her back arched and her hips bucked.

"Ooh Kenneth," Bella sighed as Kenneth swirled his tongue around her clit. "Mm-m baby."

"Wake up sleepy head," said Kenneth after he kissed her pussy goodbye.

"I'm awake now." She sat up a little bit and said, "That was downright sinful."

"Isn't it time for us to start getting ready to go?"

"No. It's time for you to get in this bed with me. Ooh or better yet the shower. That way we can save time."

"Do you want me Mommy?"

"I want you baby."

In that moment Bella realized what she really wanted and needed. She chose happiness, and no man had ever made her happier than Kenneth. She opened her mind and her heart to him as she welcomed him once again into her pussy. They laid soaking wet on a pile of towels on the bathroom floor, spent.

"I love you Bella."

"I love you too Kenneth." Bella sat up and uttered words that she thought she would never say. "Stay with me?"

"What?"

"If you love me and only me then, come home with me. Stay with me Kenneth. I'm in love with you."

≈

Footprints On The Headboard

Bella stood naked. She stared at her reflection in the oversized mirror in her plush master suite bathroom of her home. Tears rolled down her face as thoughts of Kenneth filled her mind: I still can't believe last weekend was the last time I saw him alive. We fucked like rabbits on a spring day from the moment he arrived to an hour before he departed ninety days later. The last time was in the back of the limo on the way to the airport. The more time we spent together the more the idea of his permanently moving to Arizona appealed to me. I was looking forward to his return. Hell, I didn't want him to go. I wanted him here with me. I chose him. Kenneth was my first choice, my only choice.

He was supposed to be gone for three days. I told him that we could hire someone to pack his things however he insisted on saying goodbye to his mother in person. No matter how much I tried to convince him that there was no need for goodbyes he was adamant about going back home. I remember saying, "I will send her a ticket and we can tell her together here at my house. Please don't go Baby. I have a bad feeling…"

"Don't worry Mommy. We're happy together and no one in St. Louis or anywhere else in this world can change that." He kissed her soundly. "Do you love me?"

"Yes."

"Then trust me Bella."

"I do trust you Kenneth. Hurry back to me my love." Bella kissed his lips sweetly. "I love you so much."

Kenneth Lovejoy died three days after returning to St. Louis, Missouri from a bullet wound to the head. His plane ticket was purchased. His bags were packed. Kenneth went to the old neighborhood to drop off his car to his mother when he was gunned down by a stray bullet during a drive-by shooting just moments after he told his mother he loved her and gave her one final hug and kiss goodbye. Kenneth had only taken two steps away from her. He turned back one last time to wave goodbye as the cabdriver placed his luggage in

94

the trunk of the taxi. He smiled, he was happy when the bullet struck him in his right ear and blew out of his left temple killing him instantly. Kenneth's blood splattered all over his mother's pink jogging suit. She cried out in horror as she witnessed her only son's murder. The first person she called was Bella, someone else called the police.

CHAPTER EIGHT
SEDUCED BY SATAN

Heartbreak can change a person forever, and for Bella it changed her in the worse way. She became emotionless and sexually listless. She drifted through life. She refused to feel anything for anyone. Bella lost her best friend, the only man on earth who had never been unkind to her in any way, by word or deed. To hell with anyone else including Samson, she thought. She could not make herself available to him or any other man for that matter. Before long Samson married Savanna and moved away, he was stationed in Japan, which was perfect for Bella.

Just as heartbreak can change a person forever so can hope. Bella never believed in love at first sight until she laid eyes on Roman. She knew the devil could be tricky and therefore was a firm believer in lust at first sight, hot passion, meaningless affairs, and sex just for the simple pleasure of having it. She fought her feelings for Roman with everything she had however it was a battle she was destined to lose.

She met Roman while visiting her baby sister, Malaya, who had been single and sexless in Bella's opinion for far too long. As she drove up she saw a group of men moving things into the house across the street, a convenience too perfect to pass up. Bella sprung into action the moment Malaya opened her front door.

"Come sister let's meet your new neighbors."

"What?"

"Fix yourself up a little bit and come with me." Bella said as she pushed her sister back into the house. "There's a bunch of men loading things into the house across the street."

"What do they look like?"

"Black…" Bella answered with a grin.

"Black," Malaya asked surprised, as her neighborhood housed very few African-American residences.

"Yes! Wasn't that house for sale?"

"It's been on the market for a while."

"Well then, let's go. A home owner is exactly what you need!"

"How do you know if the man who bought it isn't married?"

"He's bound to have single friends. Come on! Successful men flock together. It's very rare for them to have loser friends, loser family sure but loser friends not so much."

"Good point!" Malaya said excited.

Minutes later Bella and Malaya walked across the street smiling their brightest welcome smiles. The men stopped and stared. They gathered at the end of the driveway in front of the moving truck and admired the ladies as they approached.

"Hello neighbors," Bella began festively. She looked the men over hungrily. Her eyes stopped on the big one who stood in the back with his arms crossed. Good God who is he she wondered although she said, "I'd like to introduce you all to my sister Malaya." She continued as if she was unaffected, although her eyes kept drifting back to the mystery man. "She lives in that house right over there," she said as she pointed in its general direction.

"Hello," all of the men, except for one, said to Malaya in unison.

"Please introduce yourselves gentlemen," Bella finished.

Bella held herself still as she grew more and more nervous. Her eyes helplessly locked on the silent watchman. There he was standing still in the back of the crowd of bustling men his arms still crossed still quietly observing. Although her smile never changed a wealth of thoughts and emotions flooded her head and heart all at once: Now that's one damn sexy man. Why does he keep looking at me? I wonder if he is single? No, no men where feelings can grow.

The crowd cleared just long enough for Bella to catch a sexy full frontal albeit fully dressed. Bella took a step rearward as she thought: His dick… I can see his dick snaking down his leg. Oh my! Oh my! She had not realized she was walking backwards, retreating in fact, until she reached the edge of the drive way. He moved towards her purposely. She stopped. She was stuck, frozen, in awe of his sheer masculinity. He stopped in front of her. She looked up into his eyes. She could barely breathe.

Bella would have given anything to be able to say that that moment was the beginning of her happily ever after and that she learned to love again—true love. Alas interestingly enough she could not however she dared to hope. It was on the other hand an extremely interesting experience, a time in her life she would never regret, a time in which she learned a lot about herself. Bella knew it would not end well immediately after the first hello. She felt it in her bones.

"And what's your name?" he asked his voice was deep, alluring, and purred like a Jamaican tomcat.

This is not going to end well, her mind screamed. Run away Bella, run like the wind, yet she said, "Bella…" her voice sounded foreign even to her. It had a sweetness that she did not know she could achieve. Sensuality she knew, wantonness she was all too familiar with, however what she felt in that moment was new to her.

"Well hello Bella, my name is Roman."

"Hello Roman."

"Hi, so do you live there with your sister?"

"No I have my own house about fifteen minutes north of here."

"Who do you live with?"

"I live alone."

"No children?"

"They are adults in college living in an apartment off campus."

"You don't look that old."

"I am that old."

"What about their father?"

"Divorced four years now."

"His loss…"

"Indeed… What about you?"

"One child but my marriage is over too."

"Are you the one moving in?" Bella asked hopefully.

"No, my house is around the corner." Roman replied.

"What do you do for a living?"

"I refurbish cars." He pointed to the one parked in front of the house before he continued to speak. "That one right there was completely totaled but I put it back together like new."

"Wow, you did an excellent job."

"Which car is yours?"

"The GT right there." she pointed to the red sports car parked in her sister's driveway.

"Nice!"

"Don't be impressed. The back quarter panel flaps in the wind whenever I go over forty miles per hour," she said and laughed nervously. "My ex did me the favor of crashing it when I was in Asia two years ago and a poor job of fixing the damage."

"I can fix it," he readily offered.

And in that moment Bella's heart, mind, and pussy all agreed: I want him. Three seconds later her heart returned to its happy place tucked behind a wall of ice, her mind ran for the hills as she knew it would never workout, but her pussy decided to stay and play. Bella watched Roman down on his knees fixing her car within five minutes of saying hello, a man of action. He did a wonderful job, which impressed her. Who knew it would be fourteen months before she ever saw him again.

Bella helplessly asked about Roman every time she saw one of his friends. She thought of him everyday, all of the time. She wondered how he was doing, and if he was happy. No matter who she dated she simply could not get that sexy Jamaican out of her heart or off of her mind. She definitely wanted to get him inside of her pussy. One spring morning she called her sister almost desperate to hear some news of him.

"Hi Mala," Bella greeted her sister happily.

"Hey Bel," Malaya said easily. "What's going on witcha?"

"Nothing much, I just called."

"You will never guess who I ran into at the community mailboxes."

"I have no idea. Who," she asked.

"I saw Roman and I said hi but before he could say a proper hello he asked about you. He has been thinking about you all of this time. He made sure to give me his phone number again so that you may call him."

"Really," Bella asked unimaginably happy for the briefest of moments until she realized that her sister had been keeping them apart. "Again?"

"Yeah, I saw him a few times before but I kept forgetting to tell you."

"Give me his number please."

"It's in the car."

"I'll hold."

Bella's next call was to her lover of the moment. She quickly ended their meaningless affair hung up the phone and dialed Roman's number. He was happy to hear from her. He had almost given up hope. Bella learned that Roman had given his number to her loving sister several times over the previous fourteen months: at the grocery store, twice at the community mailboxes, and at her house while she was pulling weeds just to name a few. She also learned that her dear sister invited Roman out each time. He declined each invitation and politely asked her to give Bella his number.

Bella and Roman began the getting to know you stage of their journey together over a game of pool. She spent the whole evening lusting after him even though he drove a minivan. At the end of the evening she invited him back to her house however he never showed. She wanted to call him to make sure everything was okay but she was advised by her darling sister not to call as it would make her look desperate. The next date was a steak and lobster lunch with oysters on the half shell. Bella and Roman talked and laughed together comfortably. The third date was at his house for wine and a movie. Roman was a complete gentle man, however, Bella was more interested in him being anything but.

"You can relax Bella. I'm going to get into your head way before I try to get into your body."

We'll see about that… Bella thought although she said, "You don't say?"

"What kind of men are you use to dating?

"Men under thirty."

"You know I'm over thirty don't you?"

"Yes."

"Why do you date young men?"

"Because I can cum over thirty times in an hour and I need a man who can keep up with me. Shall I show you?"

"Yes!"

Roman grabbed Bella by the hand and rushed her to his bedroom, to hell with getting into her head first. She was delighted. She wanted to show off. She knew they would not last. She knew it would not end well from the moment she laid eyes on him and therefore she wanted to get in as much passion and pleasure as she could before it all went to hell.

Bella enthusiastically sprang into action. She slid out of her pants and panties, and all but leapt into his bed. She stretched out before him, spread her legs so that he may have an excellent view, and asked him to start counting. Before he got to the count of twenty she came. Her juices flowed over her fingers as she looked into his animated eyes. Bella's breath was slightly labored and her eyes were glossed over. She was more than thrilled. When she looked into his eyes she could tell he was excited too. He climbed into bed with her, gripped her thighs, and licked up all of her juices. She came for him over and over again. Roman wanted more.

"I want you Bella."

"You can have me Roman… if you have a condom." He didn't have one. "Damn" Bella said sweetly. "I need to clean up," she continued with a smile.

"I'll get you a towel."

Roman called the next morning, early. Bella smiled as she said hello. They shared a little small talk which she is absolutely no good at, during which she realized he had gotten the wrong impression because before she could formulate her next sentence he was saying goodbye. She however could not let the conversation end that way.

"Roman…?"

"Yes Bella?"

"I'd like you to come visit me."

"You would?"

"Yes. I want you to come over one night this week when you have some free time. You need to be well rested and have an open mind."

"Really, what are we going to do?"

"Yes really. We are going to play Bella games."

"Bella games, what's that?" Roman asked his curiosity peeked.

"You'll find out when you get here."

"Give me two days."

"All right…"

Bella gave Roman her address again before she ended the call. She spent the next two days preparing for his visit. She straightened her hair, arched her eyebrows, exfoliated her skin and pumiced her feet. On the day of she removed the hair from her underarms, legs and pussy. She had not bothered to do the latter two in years. Bella dressed carefully: black negligee, black stilettos, and a black and red oriental robe. Her makeup was flawless done in shades of berry and black with cherries jubilee lipstick. She pinned her hair up fastening it with a black and gold chopstick. She fragranced my body with her favorite scent—Japanese cherry blossom all over body spray and the matching lotion. She chilled a bottle of her favorite Moscat wine and retrieved a bottle of tequila from under the bar. She dimmed the lights, lit some candles, placed her favorite erotica movie into the DVD player, and laid a dark red fur blanket on the floor. When Roman rang Bella's doorbell at seven thirty sharp she was more than ready.

"Hello Roman," she greeted him with a sexy smile.

"Hello Bella."

"Come on in," said the spider to the fly. Bella giggled at her thought.

"What's so funny?" Roman asked as he stepped into her home cautiously.

"Nervous…" she lied. "Make yourself at home. Have a seat. Would you like something to drink?"

"Yes thank you," he said. He slipped off his shoes before following her to the living room.

"I want to share my favorite wine with you. I hope you like it." Bella poured two glasses of wine before she sat next to him. "Shall we continue on with our wine and movie night? Somehow it got interrupted before."

"By all means… Mm, this wine is great. Where did you buy it?"

"I travel to Escondido, California once a year to buy a few cases. Have you ever been to the California vineyards?"

"No but this is really good. Let me know when you plan to go again."

"I can do that. Are you ready to watch the movie?"

"Okay."

"Or… Shall we play the movie while we get to know one another better?" Bella asked calmly.

"Let's get to know each other Bella."

"Okay Roman, get naked," she said casually.

After the initial shock wore off, a full sixty seconds later, Roman stood up and removed his clothing, slowly, with his eyes fixated on Bella the entire time. Bella opened her robe, stretched out on the thick fur, and invited him to join her. Their first kiss was nothing less than fiery and passionate. Hell yeah, Bella's mind and pussy roared all the while her heart skipped a beat. *I knew it. He is everything I thought he would be from the moment I first laid eyes on him and I'm going to relish every moment of this.*

When the kiss ended all Bella wanted was more. Roman's devilishly desirous eyes held her captivated. She could not wait to see what would happen next. His hands were upon her flesh, and his lips on her skin—touching probing caressing kissing licking. *Oh this feels so right,* she mused. He took pause and looked intently into her eyes once more all the while he slid his middle finger into her pussy. Her body reacted immediately. Her vaginal muscles tightened around his finger as her pelvic floor quaked with excitement. Bella inhaled sharply. Roman removed his finger and licked it clean. His passion amazed her and it showed. He pulled her close, lowered his head between her thighs, and dove in with zeal. He ate her pussy like he was the defending champion in a pie eating contest. Elated, Bella came quickly, a soft gentle relaxing climax. Roman slurped up her juices before attacking her clitoris with vigor, shocking her senses. She tried to close her legs however he held them open. She screamed out, it was too much for her as her body thrashed about on the red fur. She gripped fists full of the pelts as she shook her head violently. Her hips levitated towards him as if they had a mind of their own. Cum gushed out of her body splashing his face and soaking the fur.

"Wait… I need to smoke after an orgasm like that," Bella just about screamed.

"Smoke it while I'm eating your pussy."

What is it about Jamaican men? Once they have you where they want you nothing is going to get in their way. For the second time in my life I am smoking a cigar while a Jamaican man is eating my pussy, mm-mm sexy. Bella smiled at her thoughts as she took a puff of her cigar. The more Bella puffed on her cigar the more she wanted to suck his dick. Visions of her tongue licking up his pre-cum danced in her head. She wondered how delicate his dick skin would be.

"Stop," Bella cried out breathlessly.

"Stop?" he asked lips glistening.

"Yes. I need something to drink."

"Now?"

"Yes, now."

"Okay…"

Bella stretched up just enough to get her glass of wine. "Do you want your glass too?" she asked.

"Sure."

"Okay." Roman lay on his side and sipped his wine. Bella barely took two sips as she waited for him to get his fill. Once he was done she took his glass and placed it back on the tray. He rolled onto his back and closed his eyes patiently waiting for her to finish. Bella eyed Roman's dick and smiled mischievously. She scooted closer to him. He opened his eyes. She held her glass high and spilled a little bit of its contents onto his flesh. "Oops, I'm so sorry," she said insincerely. "Let me get that all cleaned up." Bella's tongue traveled over Roman's flesh following the wine trail. She licked from the shaft of his dick down to his balls, and over to his inner thighs. Roman cried out in ecstasy as he sprung forward, he sat-up almost completely straight. Bella felt powerful: That did it. I am in control it is my game from this moment on. "Lay back Roman," she instructed. "Enjoy this…" She spilled more wine and slurped it all up greedily. She sucked his dick, gobbling it up using only her mouth. He practically lost his mind. She had him in a tailspin. He was quickly losing control.

Roman grabbed Bella by the shoulders and snatched her away from his dick as he roared out. "What the hell are you trying to do to me girl?"

"I just want to enjoy you Roman," Bella answered a little too innocently.

"Well now it's time for me to enjoy you again."

"Mm, good idea… Let's say we switch to tequila?"

"Good choice."

"Wonderful, how open minded are you?"

"What do you have in mind?"

"I just wanted to teach you a little something."

"I'm an old dog Bella. What could you possibly teach me?"

"Oh a little bit of this and that," she said as she poured two shots of tequila. Bella held up one glass and smiled before she took the shot. She took the other glass and inserted it into her pussy. Roman was visibly shocked. Bella flipped upside down over the arm of the couch, spread her legs, and said, "Take your shot."

Roman knelt before Bella and stared at the bottom of the shot glass peaking out of her pussy. He removed the shot glass, placed his lips over her pussy lips, lifted her up and took the shot. He was elated.

"I've never done that before. How do you get the glass to stay in there?"

"With the same muscles I gripped your finger with."

"Where did you learn that?"

"Does it really matter?"

"No…" he all but sang.

"Good."

Roman slid his dick into her velvety delta after every shot of tequila he took from her pussy. He asked Bella to squeeze it tight before removing it again. They licked and sucked and teased and pleased one another with wine and tequila until they were both completely exhausted. She glanced at the clock and could hardly believe two hours had passed. Bella so wanted Roman to fuck her. His dick was nice and long and thick and so very filling. She made every effort to stay awake however after all the tricks and orgasms she was tired. She needed to take a break.

"Here's your wine. I'll be right back. I want to take a few more puffs of my cigar but I don't want to smoke up the house," Bella said as breezily as she could muster.

"Okay Bella," he said lazily, his Jamaican accent ever so pronounced.

Bella stepped out into the cool April evening to catch a breath of fresh air. It was uncommonly nippy for a Phoenician spring night and she was stark naked. Bella did not last five minutes in the desert night air. When she stepped back in she saw Roman sleeping on her floor. She could not help but to smile. She covered him with a duvet cover and walked down the hall to the guest bedroom. She climbed into bed and dropped right off to sleep. No pillow, no covers, no moving around trying to find a comfortable position, she fell soundly to sleep the moment her body touched the bed.

The next morning she was awakened by a little noise. Someone was moving about in her home. She opened her eyes seconds before Roman appeared at the threshold of the bedroom door. There she was lying naked across the bed with one leg hanging over the side. She smiled at him immediately and righted herself onto the bed.

"Good morning Roman."

"Good morning Bella, can you do that again?"

"Yes! Count to ten…" she said as she spread her legs and reached for her clitoris. Before he got to ten her climax had begun. Bella smiled triumphantly as she showed him her wet fingers. "See."

"Oh damn…" Roman spoke slowly his timbre impassioned. "I've got to have ya." Before she knew what was happening he was on top of her pressing his dick into her flesh.

Footprints On The Headboard

"Please let me have ya Bella." His accent deepened. "Don't turn me away…" He held her tight as he pushed past the entrance, penetrating her pussy. He was too much for her… His penis was too large to press into her delta as quickly as his passions dictated. She had never experienced that level of desire in her life before. Pleasure, pain, passion, and fear, all wound up created wantonly decadent ecstasy. "My God…" he said on bated breath.

Slow down, Bella thought yet she said nothing as her orgasms began straight away. I know I'm sober, she mused. I have never cum this much ever before in my life, stone cold sober. Her body reacted to his like no other. Bella's orgasms came forth for Roman as if he was born pleasured her. In that moment, for her, his dick was crafted by ancient sex gods and enchanted by with magical fairy dust.

Roman held her steadfast. "Damn your pussy is tight," he said as he made very effort to burry his dick deep inside of her."

"Ouch!" What kind of loose pussy women have you been fucking, Bella pondered as she held on for dear life. There is no way a dick that big should be able to fall into any pussy with ease ever.

"Open up to me baby." Roman pressed on, overpowered by desire, and before long Bella's body relented. "Yes, that's it. Cum again for me baby, cum all over my dick," Roman demanded fervently.

"Yes…" Bella felt as if her hair was on fire. She felt like her skin did not belong to her and she just knew her brain was flipping about in her skull. I have been beguiled and fucked by the devil, there is no other explanation. "What are you doing to me?" Her cum flowed out of her body continuously with each and every stroke and when it was all said and done, her pussy was ruined for any other man, or so she thought.

What the fuck was that? Bella lie in the bed baffled. The same notion rolled around in her mind hours after she had said her goodbyes to Roman: I was seduced by Satan… and I cannot wait for Roman to come back and fuck me again.

Coming soon, the saga.

"Sin-Sexual"
Novella

Bella and Roman are entangled in a passion that neither one of them can deny. Roman has a secret that can destroy their lustful romance. As their desire reaches its zenith will Bella open her heart or run away from the challenges?

Read the sin filled excerpt at:

www.MissTracee.com

Made in United States
Orlando, FL
06 May 2024

46562733R00071